THE POTTER'S HOUSE BOOKS, BOOK 18

# Home another Way

A NOVELLA

VIVANT
PRESS

Minneapolis, Minnesota

Vivant Press
Home Another Way
Copyright © 2019
Brenda S. Anderson

ISBN-13: 978-0-9862147-9-0

This novel is a work of fiction. Names, characters, places, and incidents either are the product of the author's imagination or are used fictitiously. Any resemblance to actual events, locales, organizations, or persons living or dead is entirely coincidental and beyond the intent of either the author or the publisher.

Front Cover Design by T.K. Chapin
Back Cover Design by Think Cap Studios

Printed in the United States of America

18 19 20 21 22 23 24          7 6 5 4 3 2 1

# Note from the Author

The 21 books that form **The Potter's House Books** series are linked by the theme of Hope, Redemption, and Second Chances. They are all stand-alone books and can be read in any order.

Book 1: **The Homecoming** by Juliette Duncan

Book 2: **When it Rains** by T.K. Chapin

Book 3: **Heart Unbroken** by Alexa Verde

Book 4: **Long Way Home** by Brenda S. Anderson

Book 5: **Promises Renewed** by Mary Manners

Book 6: **A Vow Redeemed** by Kristen M. Fraser

Book 7: **Restoring Faith** by Marion Ueckermann

Book 8: **Unchained** by Juliette Duncan

Book 9: **Gracefully Broken** by T.K. Chapin

Book 10: **Heart Healed** by Alexa Verde

Book 11: **Place Called Home** by Brenda S. Anderson

Book 12: **Tragedy & Trust** by Mary Manners

Book 13: **Heart Transformed** by Kristen M. Fraser

Book 14: **Recovering Hope** by Marion Ueckermann

Book 15: **Blessings of Love** by Juliette Duncan

Book 16: **Until Christmas** by T.K. Chapin

Book 17: **Heart Restored** by Alexa Verde

Book 18: **Home Another Way** by Brenda S. Anderson

Book 19: **Proven Love** by Mary Manners

Book 20: **Dawn of Mercy** by Kristen M. Fraser

Book 21: **Reclaiming Charity** by Marion Ueckermann

Visit **www.PottersHouseBooks.com** for updates on the latest releases.

*To all those who see and serve the hungry and homeless*

*"There were two classes of charitable people: one, the people who did a little and made a great deal of noise; the other, the people who did a great deal and made no noise at all."*

— Charles Dickens, **Bleak House** —

*"For I was hungry and you gave me food,*

*I was thirsty and you gave me drink,*

*I was a stranger and you welcomed me..."*

Matthew 25:35

## Chapter One

*A* measly thousand-dollar fine and a hundred hours of public service? That was it? Why couldn't she have gotten ninety days in jail like any other self-respecting activist? Bringing attention to the tent city full of homeless people would be worth every minute spent behind bars and would give her cred with her activist friends. Especially with Thanksgiving only a few days away. So many people would be gorging themselves while others scrounged for mere scraps.

It wasn't fair.

Drawing her winter jacket tight around her shivering body, Dani Chamberlain kicked at the concrete of the parking ramp, following her attorney—her stubborn uncle!—to his car. When would her family allow her to grow up and handle things herself? Her mother was going to get an earful next time she saw her. But for tonight, Dani just wanted to go home, soak in the tub, and eat a container of cookie dough while watching *The Greatest Showman* for the fiftieth time.

They arrived at her uncle's Town Car, and he opened the door for her. "Done sulking yet?"

She glared at him.

And he quirked an eyebrow.

To which she shook her head. As a criminal prosecutor, Uncle Harris had received death glares from people far more intimidating than her. So, she stepped into the car and buckled her seatbelt without saying a word. Those closest to her hated the silent treatment, and as much as she felt like a child throwing a temper tantrum, silence always proved to be her most effective means of showing her dissatisfaction.

"So that's how we're going to play this." Uncle Harris closed her door, came around to his side and buckled up. Like her, he remained silent as he exited the parking ramp and turned onto the city street.

Heading in the opposite direction of her home.

What was he up to now?

She shot him a glance, which he didn't see or just ignored. Probably the latter. A few blocks later, he turned onto the freeway, taking her further away from home and her soaking tub and container of cookie dough.

She may as well give in. She cleared her throat, cobwebbed from not only the silent treatment she'd given Uncle Harris, but also from the quiet he had demanded during arraignment, the "no contest" plea, and the judge's sentence. "Where are we going? I just want to get home."

"So, she does speak."

She thought about scorching him with another glare, but it would glance right off his Teflon exterior. "Please, can you take me home?"

He grinned as he sped past a slow-moving two-person car that looked like a turtle slogging down the road. "Ah, she's employing ruthless tactics, bringing out the big guns—manners."

"I can go back to the silent treatment again."

"No, no, I wouldn't want that." He flicked on the blinker.

And her stomach turned. "Mom's?"

"The senator needs to pay my bill."

The senator . . . she hated it when her uncle referred to his sister that way, and he knew it too, which was probably why he did it. "That's what you're worried about?" She reached down to the floor for her purse then remembered she'd left it at home, per her uncle's instructions. Grrr. "I am perfectly capable of paying my own attorney fees, thank you very much."

"Are you?" He shot her an arched-brow glance as he turned onto the county road leading toward her mother's estate.

Dani wasn't going to dignify that question with an answer. She had a job—a well-paying job even, when she chose to focus on that rather than bringing attention to her pet causes. What was more important? Stuffing her pocketbook or feeding the hungry? Fact was, she did not need to rely on her mother for funds, but her mom and her uncle conveniently forgot that fact.

"Your mother requested that you join her for supper. Who am I to turn her down?"

"It's easy, actually." She pointed to the phone button on his steering wheel. "You call her up and tell her you brought her loving daughter home, and she'll join her for supper tomorrow."

"She wants to see you *tonight*."

Well, Dani certainly didn't want to see Mom tonight. She couldn't handle her disappointment. "I have a previous engagement." With her soaking tub.

"Guess you'll have to cancel it."

"No way."

"She's only home this week. Next week they're voting on key legislation."

"I'll see her on Thanksgiving."

"Dani, please . . . "

"Now who's employing ruthless tactics?" Besides, arguing with an attorney was fruitless. Why did she ever bother? But she could offer an alternative in language he understood. "How about this plea bargain? If I promise not to get into trouble for the rest of the year, you can take me home, and I'll drive to Mom's. I do have a license, you know. Have had one for six years, actually. Don't even have any tickets. You can give me a lighter sentence for good behavior."

"That's proven good behavior, which you haven't demonstrated." He grinned and scratched his late-afternoon stubble. "But still, not a bad argument. A little tweaking and you could become a good attorney."

She snorted. "Two in the family is enough." At least her brother had some sense and avoided the family business, not that being a preacher was any better.

Besides, she enjoyed selling homes, and seeing her clients' faces light up when presented with the key to their front door. Truthfully, being a realtor wasn't much different from being an attorney or a preacher: they all used their silver tongues to make a sale, be it a not-guilty verdict, a soul for Christ, or a house. "So, you'll take me home?"

"Not a chance."

"Fine." She crossed her arms and slumped in her seat, reverting back to the silent treatment. Minutes later, they drove through the gated driveway of the massive home she and her brother had grown up in and escaped from.

If only Dad were still alive, Dani would actually have someone who listened to her instead of treating her like a child.

She shook off that thought as Uncle Harris parked in front of the garage. He pushed a button on the ceiling of his vehicle and the door glided up, revealing Mom's crossover and a room full of brown storage boxes. What was that about?

"What's going on?" She gestured to the boxes.

"Don't ask me." Lawyer-speak for don't ask him because he wasn't going to reply even though he knew the answer.

"You're infuriating."

"Helen tells me the same thing."

"Aunt Helen is a saint for putting up with you."

"Don't I know it."

Dani opened the car door and felt her uncle's hand on her arm.

"Speaking of your aunt, she says it's been too long. She needs a visit and a hug from her favorite niece."

Her *only* niece. "You can tell my favorite aunt"—her only aunt—"that I'll see her soon. Maybe this weekend."

"I'll let her know. Love you, Danielle."

She sighed and shook her head. How could she stay angry with her uncle when he threw those words at her? "Love you, too." And she did, just as she loved her mom, even though their relationship went hot then cold then hot again faster than summer turned into winter. Hopefully tonight, warm words would be shared.

If only Dani would learn to curb her tongue at the right moments.

She stepped out of the car, closed the door, and gave her uncle a wave before making her way into the garage. She walked around the boxes that filled two spaces in the garage from cement floor to raftered ceiling. All were unlabeled and secured with packing tape. What was her mom up to now? Not selling the place, of that Dani was certain. Even though the estate home was far too big for only one person, it had been in the Chamberlain family for a century and was a piece of her father Mom would never relinquish. Dani didn't blame her for that, but someday, when Dani inherited the house, she'd open it to the homeless.

That would be a legacy Dad would be proud of.

She punched in the home's security code then entered the

mud room where she removed her shoes and hung her coat. No scents wafted toward her as they usually did when dining with her mom. No sound drifted toward her either.

"Hey, Mom." She walked into a spotless, lemon-scented kitchen. Mom must have ordered takeout, hopefully from that Thai place up the road. Her mouth watered just thinking about it.

The dining room, where they usually dined together, was empty. The living room was also empty. Mom wouldn't be on the second floor, which had four bedrooms and just as many bathrooms, so that left the basement family room. Dani backtracked to the stairway leading down, opened the door, and listened. Voices drifted toward her. The television. Mom was probably gearing up for the Monday evening football game. She and Dani did enjoy yelling at the screen together.

If the bathtub and cookie dough weren't calling her, Dani would stay and enjoy the game with her mom.

Going to the steps, she called out, "Hey, Mom, what's with all the—"

She jerked to a stop at the sight of her mother seated motionless as a statue on the sectional, her face angled forward, gaze focused on a framed photo on the coffee table in front of her. The last family portrait they'd had taken with her father. Beside the photo was a box of chocolates from Cheri's Chocolate Shoppe.

Oh, boy. Had Dani's latest escapades driven her mom to gorge on chocolate?

She reined in all her frustrations and questions. When her mom was in this kind of funk, seeking answers would be futile, so she'd try another tactic. Forcing a smile, she said, "I hope you saved me a chocolate-covered caramel marshmallow."

Mom's head turned her way, her expression unreadable.

"Both light and dark chocolate."

"You do love me." The chocolates had been her dad's favorites, which then, by default, became Dani's favorites as well. She sat beside her mom, selected a dark chocolate candy, and bit into it. Flavor burst on her tongue, and she sighed with pleasure. This would almost make up for not having that tub of cookie dough.

"You are so much like your father." Mom picked up the photo and shook her head. "He's been gone fifteen years. How can my heart still break over him?"

Dani reined in tears, wishing she saw this side of her mother more, the side that let her guard down and showed real emotion. If only Mom's constituents saw this woman and not the politician whose every emotion was an act. "I miss him, too."

Mom patted Dani's hand. "He always implored me not to quench your spirit, and I've done my best."

"You've done a great job." Though she hated to admit it to herself. Mom might not like her activist ways, but she'd never stood in Dani's way. Just as she'd never stopped her father from following his passions.

But if she had, would he still be alive?

Nope. Not going there.

"No, no I haven't." Mom sighed and stared at the picture again. "I haven't given you the freedom you really need. Your brother and your uncle warned me repeatedly, but I haven't listened."

A warning tingle slinked down Dani's spine. "Wait a second." She tucked herself into the corner of the sectional. "When are they going to stop butting into my life? You've always encouraged me to pursue my passions."

"Yes, yes, I have, while keeping you caged in another way. I

17

haven't allowed you the freedom to live on your own."

The woman was talking nonsense.

"What do you call living in my own apartment for the last two years?"

"I call it a cage." Mom turned to her. "A gilded cage, but a cage nonetheless. Have you ever thought about your rent? How absurdly low it is for that area?"

"Well, yeah, but . . . " But what? Dani gulped. The rental price had been way too good to be true. As a realtor, she knew that, but still hadn't questioned it.

"Or your car. What a good deal you got?"

She pressed herself tighter against the sofa's arm. "I hadn't thought about that."

Mom shook her head. "I've done exactly the opposite of what your father wanted. I've manipulated everything to keep you where I wanted you. You wanted to live downtown. I wanted you to be safe, so I made a deal with the building owners and have been paying the majority of your rent."

Dani slouched as she searched for words to express her confusion. "My car's lease payment too?"

Mom's entire body heaved with her sigh. "Yes."

"How could you?" Anger propelled Dani off the couch.

"You're my little girl. I needed to keep you safe. Your brother moved to another state and I hardly ever see him. I couldn't lose you, too. Yet, all I've done is teach you that things are handed to you. Your father would not be pleased."

"He's not the only one." Dani paced in front of the large-screen television showing players practically beating each other up, all for a silly football. "So, what now?" Did she move out of the apartment she loved? Knowing the market, she could never afford it on her own. And she loved her Lexus. She needed it for those all-important first impressions when showing homes to clients.

Mom folded her hands on her lap. "Now you find a home and a vehicle you can afford. I'll give you until the end of December to find something, then no more interference from me."

Move out by the end of December? During the holiday season when no one was moving and there would be no apartments available?

Dani stopped in front of the fireplace, mulling over her limited options. Wait . . . Those boxes in the garage . . . She turned to her mom and crossed her arms over her chest. "Did you move me out of my apartment?"

Mom looked down at the half-eaten box of chocolates. "I did."

She swallowed the marshmallow-sized lump in her throat. "And my car?"

"Returned."

Every cell in Dani's body screamed with tension. How dare Mom take away her apartment? Her car? No more interference, no more manipulating? Hah. What a lie! She was still toying with her life just as she played with her constituents'.

Mom secured the cover on the box of chocolates without looking at Dani. "You may stay in your old room until the end of December. That should give you plenty of time to find something. It's about time I let you learn to live on your own. Then you'll have the real freedom your father wanted for you."

"I won't need a month." She clenched her fists, digging long fingernails into her palms. "The less time I spend with you, the better."

Tonight, Austin Lang was going to celebrate. One trimester of teaching already under his belt! He practically skipped up the steps leading to his cozy apartment above a garage. Five years ago, he never would have imagined he'd not only have a college degree, but that he'd be responsible for molding young adults. What an awesome privilege.

He unlocked his door and entered the apartment he'd been grateful to live in for the past three years. Meeting Beatrice Dell had been a godsend, like every other event in his life recently. The studio was all he'd needed while attending school, and the homemade meals that Bea frequently graced him with also helped his budget.

But now, with a full-time teaching job, for the first time in his life he actually had some fun funds too. He dug his phone from his front pocket to call his sister and see if she'd like to celebrate with him, Skype-style. It wasn't the same as in person, but when her foster family had moved to Florida, she'd moved with them, even though she'd aged out of the foster system.

Someone knocked on his door as he brought up Brittany's number. He stuffed the phone back into his pocket and opened the door to find Bea standing there with a food storage container in her hands.

"Hey." He waved her inside. "Come on in."

She handed him the container. "Some of your favorite treats to celebrate you completing your first trimester of school."

"Thank you." Austin lifted the corner of the lid and peeked inside. The scent of chocolate escaped and made his mouth water. Cookies and fudge and bars, oh my! Good thing he had a great metabolism, or he'd swell like a hot air balloon. "Have a seat." He gestured to the daybed which at night turned into his bed. He set the goodies on the kitchen counter. "Can I get you a drink? Water? Milk? Pop?"

"I'm fine." She waved her hand. "I just want to hear about your day."

He sat in a recliner he'd found at a thrift store a few years back. "Amazing. You wouldn't believe how many kids have no clue what it takes to run a household." Not long ago, he would have been in their exact shoes. *If* he'd actually gone to high school. Being a homeless teen had put a huge crick in those plans.

"And I can't imagine anyone better at teaching them. I love how God uses our trials for His kingdom purposes."

"Amen to that." Without going through what he had as a teen, he wouldn't be half the teacher he was today.

"But I'm also afraid I have to add one more trial to your life." Her wrinkled hands folded together in her lap.

"Are you okay?" Losing Bea would be like losing his grandmother all over again.

She waved her hand. "Oh, I'm just fine, but I've been hearing from the Lord recently, and I'm not too happy with what He's telling me."

Austin shook his head. Even after living here for three years, he still wasn't used to her intimacy with God, but he'd also learned to trust that when she said she heard from Him, she had heard. The fact that it was about him stirred his gut. "What's He telling you?"

She pursed her lips and looked upward as if receiving another message, then nodded like she was agreeing with whatever the message was. "When Russell—may God rest his soul—and I added the apartment above our garage, it was intended to be for people who were needing a home, and whose finances wouldn't allow that luxury."

Which was how he'd gotten the apartment.

Oh.

Which also meant he no longer qualified. Why hadn't he seen this coming? Because he'd gotten comfortable. Complacent even, and God loved to stir him up when he got complacent.

"How long do I have?"

"Until the end of January."

Yikes! A little over two months. Between teaching Family and Consumer Science during the week and coordinating the Family Table Meal each Saturday, his calendar was already overflowing.

She sniffled and wiped a tissue over her eyes. "I always hate this part of the ministry."

"Hey, it's okay." He got out of the recliner and sat by this amazing woman who'd graciously opened her home to a stranger, as others had done for him. "I've been thinking about buying a place, you just gave me the kick I needed to start the process."

"Well, if you need a reference for anything, know you have mine." She wiped her nose. "I'll leave you be." She patted his leg and stood.

"Can I help you down?" He walked with her to the door.

"Pish. Going up and down stairs is what keeps me young. You have a good evening now." She gave him a kiss on his cheek. "And enjoy your Thanksgiving with the Brooks family."

"I will. Happy Thanksgiving to you, too." He stood on the outside landing until she made it down the thirteen steps. Then he went inside, closed the door, and leaned against it.

He had only two-and-a-third months to overcome this new problem. Yeah, he'd been looking into buying a house, that was true. What he hadn't told her was that he had too little credit history to qualify for a mortgage. For some reason, having no car payment and only one credit card that he rarely used hurt his credit. This world was messed up. But he'd faced harder challenges in the past and overcome them.

He'd overcome this problem too.

*Chapter Two*

"That gives me sixty-eight days until I have to move out." Austin handed a stack of bowls to Richard, his mentor, who placed them on the table for the meal assembly line. With the extra-cold weather, the number of homeless dining today would probably be double what he usually expected for the weekly Family Table Meal. He'd been told that just two days ago, all the seats in this church fellowship hall had been filled for the Thanksgiving meal.

"That's not much time." Richard grabbed a handful of spoons from a drawer and handed them to one of the many volunteers Austin had recruited for the day.

Austin shrugged. "It is what it is." He crossed over to the stove and checked on made-from-scratch chicken noodle soup simmering in four separate kettles. Today, the soup would be a big hit. In a few minutes, he'd start broiling the cheese sandwiches.

At least Austin had options on where to live. The majority of the people dining here today would be sleeping outside tonight.

He'd slept outside on colder nights.

Never again.

Now he'd do whatever he could to help others overcome the same situation. Richard had helped him, the least he could do was pay it forward.

He buzzed around the church kitchen, checking on each of the food stations. One group of people assembled cheese sandwiches, another mixed salad. Other volunteers prepped the tables in the fellowship hall. Additional volunteers would serve the diners as if they were at a fancy restaurant. Others would assemble food on plates and more would wash dishes. Two would man the free store where diners could choose from donated items, things most people took for granted: socks, food, soap, and more.

"Looks like you're ready." Richard slapped Austin on the back. "I'm proud of what you've done here."

Austin shrugged and grabbed a tray of sandwiches. He'd only taken over what someone else had established years ago. The hard work had already been done. After inserting the sandwich-filled tray into the broiler, he leaned against the kitchen counter and glanced at the door leading outside. People would start filtering in any time now.

"So, tell me." Richard stood beside him. "Have you done any looking online for homes?"

"I did some research yesterday. It's crazy what little apartments rent for. If I qualified for a mortgage, I'd buy a townhome. That'd be cheaper than rent."

"And you don't have enough credit to qualify, right?"

Austin snorted. "Yep."

"How about if I co-signed—"

"They tell me you're Austin Lang." A young woman butted into their conversation and handed Austin a business card. *Danielle Chamberlain, Realtor.* Seriously?

Wrinkling his nose, he squinted down at her. "We're rather busy here, and the people we serve don't have much need for a realtor."

She blinked, then a smile brightened her face. "Sorry, I'm not here looking for business. I'm here to volunteer."

Austin took in the woman standing in front of him, probably here to cross do-a-good-deed off her to-do list. Perfectly styled, reddish hair. Makeup. A fancy blouse. Jeans that looked like they'd never been worn before. Shoes with two-inch heels. A purse that probably cost more than everything he owned. "Dressed like that?"

"I was told to dress for work."

She had to be kidding.

Out of the corner of his eye, he watched Richard cover a smirk with his hand.

"Yeah, hard work. As in you'll be on your feet for the next four to five hours, serving, doing dishes, cleaning."

She crossed her arms, her purse slinging from her elbow, and bore her gaze into his. "I know that."

*Idiot.* He mentally slapped the side of his head. Rule number one for getting volunteers to work was to not insult them the moment they stepped through the doorway.

He raised both hands, signaling his surrender. "I'm sorry. That was wrong. Let's start over." He offered his hand. "I'm Austin Lang, coordinator of Saturday's Family Table Meal."

She smiled back. "Dani Chamberlain, volunteer extraordinaire. You'll be glad I'm here." She rolled up the sleeves on her blouse, as if that gave her credibility.

Uh-huh.

"Oh, and . . . " She dug into her purse and pulled out a piece of paper. "When we're done today, I'll need you to sign off on my time. I plan to be here every week until my hours are complete."

Ah, now it made sense. She was one of those community

service "volunteers." Well, he'd put her to work, all right. Dishes and food assembly would be too easy. But service. That would get her to interact one-on-one with the diners, most of whom smelled like they hadn't showered in a month. They probably hadn't. If she wanted him to sign off on work done, she was going to earn every hour.

"Okay then, I'll introduce you to Joe. He's in charge of the servers and will let you know what you need to do."

He introduced Dani to a man who bore a striking resemblance to Santa Claus then returned to Richard, who no longer hid his smirk.

"What would you have done?" Austin splayed his hands.

"Exactly what you did." Richard nodded to the woman. "She's rather cute, don't you think?"

Austin shrugged while looking at her. "I guess." Well, she really was cute, but showing up here dressed like that told him she didn't have a lot of functioning brain cells. Intelligence was far more attractive than looks.

"You don't know who she is, do you?"

"Should I?"

"Maybe you need to pay more attention to the news." Richard punched at his phone then showed Austin a picture of Dani with the headline, *Senator Felicity Chamberlain's Daughter Sentenced.*

Austin groaned. "The senator's daughter?"

"The one and only, and everything I hear about her says she's a handful. Aren't you the lucky one?"

"Yippee." He watched the first of the diners amble into the fellowship hall and laughed. He couldn't wait to see how fancy Dani handled stinky Larry.

Oh, that went well. Dani rolled her eyes while hiding her purse in a kitchen drawer. No one had told her to leave her purse behind, and was it her fault she didn't have any ratty clothes to wear? Sheesh! Yet, by the reception she'd been given from Austin and Joe, a Santa Claus lookalike, one would think she had leprosy. She'd show them.

A stench preceded the man who entered the dining hall. Dani's eyes watered and she did her best to keep down her breakfast.

*He's a person, a child of God just like me, and he deserves to be treated as such.* Dani summoned her make-the-sale smile and strode toward the man who beneath the grime looked to be in his twenties. What was his story? How did he end up on the streets?

She didn't offer her hand, but instead gestured toward the tables while trying not to breathe in. "Welcome to Family Table. Can I show you to a seat?"

"I know where to go." He trudged past her and sat at a table nearest the kitchen.

Okay then.

She called back her smile and approached him again. "May I offer you a beverage? Water? Juice? Coffee? The meal will be served in about ten minutes."

"Coffee," he said without looking at her.

"Be right back."

Three hours later, Dani plopped down on a chair by a newly-deserted table, exhausted. She removed her shoes and rubbed her feet. Tonight, she'd relish the tub at her mom's place.

But would she be able to relax knowing that the people she'd just served not only didn't have access to a bathtub, but also a shower? What she'd done today, feeding them one meal, was only a bandage on what they really needed. If only her mom could see that and approve legislation to help, she could make a real difference.

Dani put on her shoes, got up, and walked around the emptying fellowship hall, carrying a tray filled with leftover chocolate cake. Most diners had left already, which broke her heart. The temperature was hovering around ten above and this winter seemed to be colder than ever. For the sake of those who dined here, Dani hoped for a warm winter. She even lifted a prayer or two for them. Her mom and brother would be pleased.

With two slices of cake remaining on her tray, she angled for the back corner of the room, toward a woman wearing an oversized trench coat, who kept to herself. By the hunch of her back, the woman looked middle-aged, but it was difficult to judge fairly without seeing her face.

Dani stood across the table from the woman. "Care for a piece of cake?"

No answer, so Dani set the extra piece down in front of the woman, who instantly grabbed it.

"Mind if I sit here?" Dani pointed to an empty chair across from the woman.

The woman sighed so hard her shoulders sighed with her. "Suit yourself."

"Thanks." Dani sat and cut a bite-sized piece of cake while peering through her lashes at the woman. "I'm Dani."

"Good for you." The woman shoved a forkful of cake into her mouth, but that didn't cover the alcohol on her breath, something Dani had noticed on many of the diners. "Do you have a name?"

"Nope. My mom forgot to give me one."

Okay then. Dani would have to take a different route. "You look like a Samantha. Mind if I call you Sammi?"

"I mind you talking to me." Finally, the woman looked up.

Dani stifled a gasp. This woman wasn't middle-aged, but more likely a twenty-something. What had happened in her life that sent her to the streets and aged her so? Didn't she have family or friends to take her in? Living on the streets, how did she, or any of the people here, have money to purchase booze?

And why couldn't Dani's mom pass legislation to get everyone off the street? Build affordable housing? Something? Didn't everyone deserve a home? Food? Especially during a Minnesota winter when a night spent outside could easily mean death.

"You still here?" The woman's raspy voice broke into Dani's musing.

"Just trying to be a friend."

"I got enough friends. Go annoy someone else."

"I'm sorry to bother you." Not really, though. Sammi, or whoever she was, needed someone to love on her, to be a true friend, and that was exactly what Dani planned to do. "I'll leave you alone." For today, but next week she'd be back working on winning over Sammi and a handful more that Dani had targeted, and she'd prove to her mom and her uncle that she was more than a flighty, spoiled millennial. If it took her through the entire community service hours, she'd get Sammi to open up and get her off the streets.

Then people would look up to Dani like they looked up at her mother.

# Chapter Three

"Tired?"

Dani glanced way up into Austin's blue eyes. She was tall at five foot eight, but he towered a good five inches above her. The guy looked about her age, but wisdom and empathy oozed from his being. What was his story? She intended to learn that, too.

"Exhausted." She sighed and looked toward the door all the diners had exited through into the frigid air. "My heart breaks for everyone I served today. I just want to take them all home where they can shower and eat and live life like the rest of us do."

"If only it were that easy." Austin pulled up a chair across from her and sat. "You have a form you need me to sign?"

"Oh, yes. It's in my purse . . . which I promise not to bring next week." She hurried to the kitchen, praying her purse was still in the drawer and that it hadn't been looted. She tugged open the drawer and released a breath as she removed the purse and took a quick inventory. Nothing had been stolen, that she was aware of anyway. Judging from tales she'd heard today from other volunteers, she was fortunate.

She sat across from Austin, who was chatting with that same guy who'd been with him in the kitchen. Interrupting wasn't polite, but she needed to get home and cleaned up. Saturday was her busiest day as a realtor and now more than ever, she needed to make sales if she wanted to live in a decent place. She couldn't believe how expensive it was to rent a one-bedroom apartment with no amenities.

No wonder people were homeless.

"Excuse me, Austin." She slid her community service form and a pen across the table as Austin mentioned something about finding a realtor. She bit her tongue, preventing an inappropriate sales pitch. "Would you mind signing this?"

"Sure." He smiled and penned his signature. "I'll see you next Saturday?"

"I'll be here." She gestured toward her outfit. "And I'll be more appropriately dressed."

"Hey, I'm sorry about that. I was rude. Arrogant. I know how it feels to have people look down on me, and then I did the same thing to you. Forgive me?"

"I, uh, yes. Of course, I forgive you." Flustered, Dani took the service form and started to stand, but then she had an idea and sat back down. "I have another question."

"Okay . . . "

"Is there any other way for me to serve? This was—is—wonderful, but it seems so . . . " She shook her head. How to phrase it without belittling the benefits of the meal. "I just feel I need to do more."

"Like when you were collecting food for the homeless on the side of the freeway?" Austin crossed his arms.

"I, uh." She sighed. "Yes, like that, but something legal."

The two guys laughed.

"Well, at least you have heart." Austin folded his hands on the table. "Tomorrow after church I'm going with a group to that tent city that's sprung up north of Amery. You're welcome to join us."

"Let me check my schedule." She pulled her phone from her purse and brought up her schedule. Shoot, she was working an open house tomorrow afternoon. "I'm busy tomorrow, but in the future, I'd love to go."

"Great. I'll keep you posted."

"You know how to reach me?"

He dug her business card out of his pocket. "I'm assuming this works."

"Oh, yeah." Her cheeks warmed with embarrassment. "But how do *I* get in touch with *you*?"

He pulled out his wallet, took out a business card, and handed it to her.

"You teach FACS?"

"Sure do."

"Nice." Why that surprised her, she didn't know. Just because all her Family and Consumer Science teachers had been female didn't mean that men couldn't teach it. Judging by how he ran this meal, he was undoubtedly a very good teacher. She pocketed his card. "We'll be in touch."

"Oh, and I was wondering, too . . . " Austin scratched the back of his neck. "Looks like I'm gonna be doing some house hunting, and I could use a good realtor. You know one?"

She grinned. "I happen to know a very good one. I believe you have my card."

"I do." He showed it to her. "But I also plan to do research on a couple more realtors before making a commitment."

"As you should." She burrowed into her purse again and pulled out a business card for a mortgage lender she recommended. "But before you do any searching, I suggest getting pre-approved for a mortgage. No matter which realtor you go with, it'll make the whole process go smoother."

"That's what Richard was telling me." He nodded sideways to the gentleman sitting beside him.

"You must be Richard." She extended her hand across the table to the man who'd silently watched their exchange.

"Richard Brooks." He gripped her hand solidly. "Austin's like a son to me, so I'll be advising him on the house hunt."

The steel in his eyes warned her she would not want to mess with him or Austin.

She then offered her hand to Austin. "I look forward to working with you." No, he hadn't confirmed, but it was a psychological tactic she'd been taught to use. "Just call me when you're ready to start."

"And I'll let you know if I go with someone else."

"Of course." She grinned. "Regardless, I'll see you next Saturday."

Dani picked up her purse and strode from the dining hall, trying to wrap her mind around who this Austin was. Except for their very first encounter, he'd come across as compassionate. He really loved the people he served here.

Could he be someone worth getting to know better?

Guess she'd figure that out over the coming weeks.

"Well that was interesting."

Austin looked sideways at Richard. "What are you talking about."

"Just a feeling." He shrugged. "And a warning to be careful around Ms. Chamberlain. She's a bit of a powder keg. Her recent arrest isn't the first time she's made the papers. Yeah, she's fighting for the little guy, but her motives are in question. Is she an activist in rebellion against her mother—something I'm very familiar with—or does she really have a heart for the homeless?"

ˡ "If she's helping people, does her motive matter?"

"It does if she pulls others down with her, and you've worked too hard to get where you are for her to drag you back down."

"Warning noted." Besides, he had no time for a relationship, especially with someone as high maintenance as a senator's daughter. It would never work out.

"Good." Richard slapped Austin on the back. "Then let's get out of here and begin that house-buying process."

Dani greeted her mother then hurried up to her room to change into something clean. She had planned to head straight to her showings in the clothes she'd worn to the meal, but after getting spilled on several times, and working up a sweat, her current outfit was going right to the dry cleaners.

If only she could volunteer during the week and not on the weekends. How was she supposed to support herself and fulfill all her service hours? How was she supposed to find a home for herself?

How dare she whine after today?

She looked outside at the wind-whipped trees. Even in a tent, or a cardboard box, the homeless would be cold. And hungry. Sure, she'd been kicked out of her apartment, but she wasn't really homeless or hungry. The night she and fellow protesters slept in cardboard boxes had been more of an adventure than a hardship. She would never really know what being homeless felt like.

Her mom and brother would tell her to pray.

Austin probably would, too.

She did, at times, but praying hadn't come easy since her dad had been murdered.

She put on dress pants and a sweater and hurried downstairs and out the front door to her *new* vehicle, a ten-year-old Lexus.

How could she make a difference in the world when she'd been too blind to see the luxury she'd been given?

That wasn't a problem she could solve today. Today was about finding homes for people who could afford them, and that was important too.

Her phone sang as she pulled out of the long driveaway. She hit the button on her steering wheel to answer it.

Only, that button didn't exist on this car. Rats. She'd have to rig up something so she could talk and drive at the same time since she spent much of her job in the car. Several additional callers attempted to reach her before she arrived at the showing. Her clients weren't there yet, so she retrieved her phone from her purse and brought up her voice mail. Only two messages.

The first informed her that the clients weren't late. No, they weren't going to show at all. No reason given. And this wasn't the first time they'd pulled that on her. If only she could pass their business on to someone else. She was tired of them wasting her time, but she desperately needed the commission.

The second message said her open house for tomorrow was cancelled due to sickness in the family.

And that was the extent of her client list right now. On top of there being a lull in the housing market during the holiday season, she'd been more focused on making the news than finding new clients. Until she'd received the eviction notice from her mom, that hadn't been an issue.

Which left tomorrow afternoon open. She could go with

Austin to the tent city. Maybe there she could learn how to make a real difference in the world.

## Chapter Four

*a*ustin lifted a prayer that God would give him wisdom this afternoon, and that He would keep them all safe. Then he hurried to the living room at Our Home, a house for homeless teens. Several volunteers for the day had gathered there, many of whom were residents of Our Home and had experienced homelessness firsthand. He did a quick count. Ten volunteers, eleven including himself, the biggest group he'd had yet.

His gaze immediately flew to Dani Chamberlain seated cross-legged on the floor. She'd dressed down from yesterday, but she still carried an air of regality about her. Even if she wore rags, she'd stand out.

She smiled at him—a pretty nice smile at that—and he dragged his gaze away, while clearing his throat.

"Thanks, everyone, for signing up to join us today. Remember, our aim isn't to proselytize, but to be Jesus to those at the camp. We need to see them not as homeless people, but as children of God, and He loves them just as much as He loves each of us."

A volunteer raised her hand. "Does that mean we're not supposed to talk about Jesus at all?"

"No, no it doesn't. It just means we're not to cram Him down people's throats. Do what comes naturally to you. For some of us that means talking. For others, it means simply handing someone a pair of wool socks."

"Why wool?" A young man asked.

"Wool socks last longer. Hold the heat in better. They can absorb a lot of moisture. And, as you know, if your feet are cold, your entire body's cold."

"What else can we expect going there?" This from Dani.

"Good question." Austin leaned against the wall. This was always the toughest part in going to the camp. "Expect nothing."

Silence filled the room, and he stood up straight. "Our job isn't to change hearts—that job belongs to God and God alone. Our job is to show people who He is. When we pass out items, you'll be watched, analyzed, usually with a very cynical eye. They can spot a do-gooder a mile away. They're suspicious, and rightly so, because they've been used by the very people who promised to help them. So, they don't trust you, and you shouldn't trust them."

He cleared his throat, and Dani offered to get him a glass of water. She returned quickly, and he drank half the glass without a break. Speaking in front of adults always unnerved him. But as Richard had often told him, following your passion didn't mean you'd love everything you did. It just meant that doing the hard stuff was easier knowing it helped you follow your dream.

He set the glass on an end table and continued his spiel. "Don't bring any valuables. As many of you know, since you've been homeless, some of the people living in the camp are just down on their luck. Like many of you, maybe they've aged out of foster care. Or else they've lost a job and haven't found one yet. For some, the cost of housing is just too high."

Austin downed the rest of his water, while mentally preparing for the real tough part of his speech. He set down the glass and made sure he connected gazes with each volunteer in the room. They needed to know the gravity of the situation they were walking into. "But all those are in the minority. Many living in the camp are there of their own choosing. Some have mental health issues. A majority have serious drug and/or alcohol problems. Others are running from the law for various reasons such as being in the country illegally, burglary, selling drugs, rape." He paused for added effect. "Murder."

Gasps were heard from some in the room, likely those who hadn't experienced homelessness firsthand.

"So, is it safe to go?" A young woman draped her sweater tightly around herself as if trying to hide. She had good reason.

"The honest answer is no. And yes. Stay with the group at all times, and never go off on your own. If you do, you won't be able to join us again. No exceptions. Also, never ever go down there alone. I can't stress that enough. Going alone is asking for trouble. Don't go there at night either. Going in the daylight, in a large group, is relatively safe. If you've changed your mind about going today, that's not a problem. We all get it. No judgment."

He quieted so that information would sink in. He hated scaring off people, but he couldn't lie to them either. In all the times he'd taken a group down there, they hadn't had a problem, but he'd heard from others who weren't as fortunate.

"I'm heading out to the bus now." He glanced at his watch. One fifteen. "We're leaving at one thirty sharp. If you're not on the bus, we'll assume you're not joining us. Again, no judgment. Take a minute to use the restroom. If you have valuables, Nancy, Our Home's administrator, will lock them in her office. See you at the bus in fifteen minutes."

He put on his winter jacket, gloves, and boots then hurried

out to the bus and checked the supplies. Donations from local churches and area residents filled the back end. He'd once believed that people didn't care. Now, he knew differently. He prayed that those they met today would see the hearts of the givers. He also prayed that God would give volunteers discernment when distributing the donations.

Then he took a seat in the front of the bus, behind the driver.

Now came the wait-and-see game. He always lost a couple of volunteers, and he certainly didn't fault them. Going to a homeless camp tended to be way out of people's comfort zone. Including his, but he knew it was the right thing to do, and he was going dressed in the armor of God.

Over the next fourteen minutes, the volunteers trickled onto the bus. At one twenty-nine, all but two had boarded: the young woman with the sweater, which didn't surprise him, and Dani, which did. Not that he blamed her, he'd just assumed a trip like this was the type of adventure she sought. He checked his watch again, then the front door of the house. No sign of either, so he rapped the driver on the shoulder. "Time to go."

The bus started up, and Austin looked back at the passengers. Nine people going down was more than enough to hand out items to camp residents.

"Stop! They're coming!" Someone behind Austin yelled as the bus jerked to a stop at the end of the driveway. He looked out the window and watched Dani running alongside the young woman.

Huh.

The bus door whooshed open and Dani climbed in after the other woman. Breathing hard, she dropped into the seat behind Austin and heaved a big sigh. "I didn't think we were going to make it."

"I didn't think you were coming."

"Really? I wouldn't miss this for anything." She leaned over the seat in front of her and lowered her voice so only Austin could hear. "I just had to reassure Olivia that we'd be okay, that I wouldn't leave her side. I have a feeling there's more to her than what we see."

"There usually is."

"So that means there's more to you than a do-gooder teacher?"

He snorted as the bus started up again. "Much more." If only she knew. "What about you? I know there's more to you than what the world sees, than what the papers tell."

"You do? Well you'd be a first," she said with heavy amount of sarcasm.

"I'm sorry about that."

"For what?"

"It can't be easy living in a fishbowl, the press announcing what you had for dinner, who you went on a date with, where you took your last vacation."

"The thing is, most of the time I've sought that out. My mom did a good job of hiding me away. Me? I tend to seek out the spotlight, whether it's for good or bad. I don't know what that says about me."

"I couldn't tell you, but God knows. Ask Him."

"You sound like my brother."

"Is that a good thing?"

"It's a . . . thing." She turned away from him and looked out the window.

What had he done wrong?

Didn't matter. This trip wasn't about him or her or any of the volunteers on this bus. It was about being Jesus to broken people. Five years ago, Richard and his wife had shown him

Jesus. Today was about *praying* that forward.

He opened his hands on his lap, closed his eyes, bowed his head, and prayed silently. "Lord, You know who we're supposed to meet today. Help them to lay down whatever's holding them captive. Open their hearts so that they may see You, hear You, feel You. And offer divine protection of those with me today. We know the devil's waging war down there, but You're the victor. Amen."

Austin opened his eyes, but something niggled at him. Usually prayer took away that worry. Guess that meant he needed to remain in prayer.

And he did for the rest of the drive.

The bus backed onto a dead end that led to the tent city. Apprehension mixed with excitement in Dani's gut. She knew more about the dangers of a camp such as this than people realized. She'd lost more from one too. Back at the house she'd lied to Austin. It wasn't Olivia who needed coaxing—rather, Olivia had to convince her.

Now was an opportunity to prove to herself that she'd forgiven the woman who'd taken her father's life.

She followed the others off the bus, into air that froze words into clouds, and Austin led the group in another prayer. She'd noticed that he'd spent the entire bus ride in prayer as well. The guy definitely lived what he preached. Too bad her brother lived so far away, he'd likely get along very well with Austin.

Austin opened the back door of the bus revealing boxes and bags full of daily use items that she took for granted. Blankets, jackets, gloves, soap, socks, food, women's hygiene, and more.

Why hadn't she thought of bringing anything with her to contribute? Next time. Assuming there would be a next time.

A man who didn't look like he belonged in the camp approached the bus. Austin met him and shook his hand. The two conversed for a few minutes as people slowly emerged from their tents and made their way toward the bus. Dani swallowed hard and her heart pumped faster than shoppers racing for sales on Black Friday.

The man left, and Austin turned back to the group. "Okay, this is it. Remember, stay here. No going off on your own or you're done. Do not give money to anyone. Be yourself. Show kindness, and let God work in their hearts."

Show kindness. What did that mean anyway? Did she let people approach her, or did she take the first step?

She looked around for Olivia, but she was already talking with someone from the camp. Okay then.

She shook out her arms, trying to shake off her jitters. It didn't work, so that meant push through them. She inhaled and exhaled slowly a few times then eyed the people crowding in front of the bus, wearing threadbare clothes and jackets. Most didn't have mittens or gloves, and their footwear had more holes than Swiss cheese.

Austin had recommended just being themselves, which meant she'd go to them.

Directly in front of her, a small child clung to a woman's ratty skirt, and Dani's heart broke. She grabbed a few items from the bus and aimed for the woman whose shoulders were stooped like someone who'd lived many years. Studying her face, aged from possible drug use, Dani couldn't discern how old she was.

Dani didn't smile at her—she felt like that would be forcing a sale—rather she showed her a couple of hard-boiled eggs and nodded to the child. "May I?"

The woman gave a slow nod.

Dani knelt on the snow-packed ground, opened her hand, and smiled. "Would you like an egg?"

The girl's eyes grew as wide as the eggs, and she grasped both. "Can I help—"

The child ran off before Dani could finish her question. But the woman stayed behind, her lips pursed and arms crossed. "What have you got?"

"Eggs, tampons, water." She listed only a few items, knowing they had to serve hundreds of people. She showed the woman a drawstring bag. "You can have this to carry it in."

"Soap?"

"Yes, we have soap."

"Well, are you going to get it? Or do I have to serve myself?"

Dani bit her tongue and hurried back to the bus. Austin had told them to expect nothing, well he was certainly right about that. She added a bar of soap, several tampons, a couple bottles of water, and a couple of eggs to the bag then hurried back.

The woman grabbed the bag and hustled away without a word.

Next Dani spoke with an older man who reeked of marijuana and asked for cookies. She gave him granola bars with chocolate chips.

Then she met someone who she had no clue whether they were a man or woman and they asked for socks.

Blankets flew from the bus. Socks were the most requested item, followed by bars of soap, eggs, and water. By the end of two hours, the back of the bus was empty.

As was she.

Exhausted, she leaned against the side of the bus. Her heart was shattered. So many hurting, lost people who would be sleeping outside tonight. Some had the *luxury* of being in a tent or a cardboard box. Austin had told them many chose the life, oftentimes because shelters had too many rules. She couldn't fathom choosing a tent over a warm bed because of no-drug, no-booze rules. She couldn't imagine a chemical holding that strong of power over someone.

Her mom had told her housing the homeless wasn't as easy as building a shelter. Now she finally understood. These people needed hope that she doubted their gifts of food and clothing provided. They needed—

"Help, please! My grandfather, he's unconscious!"

Dani leaped to her feet and scrambled after the teen who didn't look like he belonged in this camp.

"Dani, get back here." Austin called out.

But she refused to stop. Someone needed help, and she would not stand by and wait for someone else to take action.

"Dani." Austin grabbed her arm, slowing her. "Stop. Medics are coming."

She stopped, just long enough for Austin to relax, then she took off after the teen again, weaving among tents, slipping on icy ground, and leaping over sleeping bags.

Up ahead people circled. Austin ran past her and broke through the crowd. She followed and gasped. On the ground up ahead lay an elderly man. Austin checked the man's airway, his breathing, and pulse. "He's not breathing." He began chest compressions while humming "Stayin' Alive."

Dani hovered over Austin, itching to kneel down and help. "What can I do?"

He fixed her with a glare that she took to mean, "Don't move." She gulped and hugged herself. What seemed like an hour later, paramedics broke through the crowd and took over for Austin, who shook his head.

Then his eyes focused on her, and the darkness in them told her he was not happy. He jutted his finger toward the bus and said, "Go."

"But what about him?" She looked back at the unconscious man. How could she leave when she didn't know if he would live?

"Now." Austin growled.

"Fine." She moved forward but kept looking back. "Do you think he'll live?"

"Probably not."

"Then what happens? Will they have a funeral? Where will he be buried?"

"It all depends upon if they have family or anyone who claims them." Gripping her arm securely, Austin steered her around the perimeter of the camp rather than through it, walking alongside the freeway sound barrier. "I do know of pastors who hold services for them, a church that will add their name, if known, to a plaque in their cemetery."

"And that's it."

Austin shrugged. "That man looked like he had family. Chances are he chose this life. But it doesn't make his death any less heartbreaking for the family, rather it compounds it."

"Something has to be done."

Austin stopped and stared at her. "Like what? Churches and local groups are here all the time, making donations, so much so that they have a pile of clothes that will never be used. The government's brought in porta-potties and portable showers. Area churches have supplied heaters for the main meeting places. Counselors come here often. They're given information on organizations that can help them give up drugs. Their plight has been in the newspaper, and Minnesotans have responded very generously. What more can we do?"

"My mom could do something."

"I don't know. Seems to me that government programs have too many conditions to be helpful."

She sniffled and wiped her eyes. "It just doesn't seem right."

"No. It doesn't. But do know that you made a difference today. It might not be visible, and we'll likely never see the results for ourselves, but our little group made an impact. We were God's hands and feet today. It's up to Him to reveal His heart."

"But will He? I have my doubts."

"Trust me, I've seen miracles happen firsthand and it's up to me to pray it forward."

She stopped next to a tent, and Austin pushed her to keep moving.

"Don't you mean *pay* it forward?"

"Nope." They finally reached the outskirts of the camp, just a few yards from the bus, and Austin came to a stop. "Everything I do is bathed in prayer, before, during, and after. No, I take that back. It's my desire to bathe everything in prayer—I'm not quite there yet. Too often I like to take things into my own hands."

"Like me running off after that teen?"

He laughed. "Yeah, like that. You have a good heart, Dani, but don't let it rule you. The head and heart have to work together."

"That's what my brother tells me."

"You should listen to him."

"That's what my mother tells me."

"Sounds like you have a lot of people telling you what to do."

She laughed. "You'd think they'd learn that I don't listen well." She aimed for the bus, her heart still aching.

Austin stepped in front of her and blocked her way, his legs spread and arms crossed. "Listening is an important tool, Dani."

"I know." She tried going around him, but he kept blocking her. "I promise I'll listen next time."

"There can't be a next time. You didn't follow the rules. I said, under no circumstances do you take off on your own. I will not have someone on my watch injured because they can't follow the rules."

"So, you'd have let that man die?"

He sighed and ran a hand through his hair. "Protocol was followed. The second that teen told us about his grandfather, our bus driver was on the phone calling 911. Medics are close by. It's not a perfect system, but it works. Just like it worked today."

"I don't get a second chance?"

"If I give you a second chance, what do I tell everyone else? That you can break the rules and get away with it? Not happening."

"Fine." She shoved past him then looked back, hoping her eyes were skewering him. "Does that mean I'm done at the Family Table Meal too?"

"Only if you come dressed like you did last time."

She raised her hands. "Is this outfit okay?"

"Much better."

"I'll see you Saturday then."

"Right. And don't be late."

Austin blew out his breath as he watched Dani get on the bus. Boy, he couldn't remember someone getting under his skin like her. She'd be the death of him before the end of her community service.

"She's a handful, son." One of his older volunteers laid a hand on his shoulder.

"Tell me about it."

"Girlfriend?"

"Nah, just someone who cares."

"Hmm. Sounds like she might be a good catch, then." The volunteer headed to the bus.

Yeah, Dani would be a good catch for someone who had time to devote to her. Extra time was something he didn't have. Besides, a senator's daughter would not be interested in an ordinary guy like him, not when she probably had her pick of men.

## Chapter Five

*A*ustin plopped down on his daybed, exhausted after the busy weekend and then the long day of work. The students had been unruly and disrespectful. Or maybe they were riled up from the long holiday weekend. Whatever the case, today had rubbed a little bit of the luster off his teaching job. But that was okay—he knew how to handle life better when it wasn't polished to a sheen, because that polish too often masked imperfections.

Regardless, tonight all he wanted to do was turn on the TV and watch a little football. For supper he'd make popcorn. He leaned back on his sofa, cradling his head in his hands. Ahh, the bachelor life.

His phone sang a generic tone, telling him it wasn't someone he knew. He pulled his phone from his pocket but didn't answer. If it was important, they'd leave a voice mail.

And now, since he'd been disturbed, he might as well make supper. He took out his microwave bowl and poured in a quarter cup of popcorn and a drop of oil. Then he nuked it for three minutes twenty-three seconds, which gave him the perfect balance of popped, unburnt kernels. He added a couple pats of butter and supper was ready.

He sat in his recliner this time, with the TV remote and phone to his left, and the popcorn and pop to his right. Now this was the life. He got settled just as Green Bay kicked off. He couldn't wait to watch them lose.

Oh, he forgot to check if someone left a voice mail. With popcorn in one hand, he awoke his phone with the other. There was a message. He hit the icon to listen:

"Hello, Austin, this is Lissa Johnson with Hennepin Bank and Trust. We've reviewed your mortgage application and would like to speak with you further. I'll be in the office until eight this evening." She left a number for her direct line as well.

Hoo boy, this was it. He lifted up a prayer that he'd be approved then returned the call to Lissa.

"This is Lissa Johnson. How may I help you?"

"Hey Lissa, this is Austin Lang returning your call."

"Austin, hello. Thank you for calling back. We reviewed your revised application today, and with your co-signer you've been approved for a generous amount, but—"

"No, no, no. I don't want to go any higher than the amount I told you."

"Exactly what I was going to suggest. You won't get much of a house, but you'll be able to afford it and you'll start building equity."

"So, does that mean I can start looking for homes?"

"Yes, as long as you realize that a pre-approval has not gone through the final underwriting process yet."

"So, I could still be denied?"

"There's always that possibility, but if you keep handling your finances as you have so far, I don't foresee a problem. I'll email the pre-approval letter to you. Once you sign a purchase agreement, plan on fifteen to forty-five days to close, depending upon how well you and your co-signer do your homework. Good luck on your home search."

"Thank you."

Austin did a little dance right there in his recliner. Step one done, but now he needed to find a home, and at the price he was willing to pay, there weren't many options, especially this time of year. No one wanted to move at Christmastime. The question now was, which realtor should he call?

The one Richard recommended to him?

Or Dani?

Logic would tell him to go with Richard's recommendation, but he knew Dani—sort of—and loved her passion. Would that make her good at her job? Maybe.

There was a way to check. He googled her name but wasn't prepared for the number of hits. Mostly stories about her too-public personal life. A lot of social activism showed her heart was pointed in the right direction but tended to go off course. She just needed to nudge it a little to stay on the right path—and out of jail.

Guess he needed to refine his search a bit. Rather than go directly to her company page, which would only show her glowing results, he did a google search of her name plus her company to see if she had any online reviews.

A whole new set of sites popped up. Now he was getting somewhere.

For the most part, she had four- or five-star reviews, the one problem he saw was that her clientele was way out of his league. Would she even consider working for him?

He did the same search on the person Richard recommended and discovered that he wasn't any different from Dani in that he typically took on the wealthy client, which certainly wasn't Austin.

"Okay, God." He looked toward the ceiling. "What do I do?"

He flipped back and forth between the two realtors but stayed longer on Dani's page. Would she treat him like her million-dollar clients, or give him her crumbs? Wouldn't hurt to ask, right?

He dialed her number, and she answered after a few rings. "Austin?" Huh, she must have his number in her phone already.

"Yeah, it's me. I have a few questions for you, if you're available right now."

"Not a problem. I just finished supper with my mother and was going to start a home search for myself."

"You need a home, too?"

"Yeah, well, turns out my latest adventure didn't exactly make my mom proud, so she's teaching me a life lesson."

"Oh, wow, I'm sorry."

"Yeah, me too." She laughed. "I had a sweet deal that I blew, and now I get to live like the average Jane."

Probably not true, but he let that slide.

"So, did I hear correctly, that you're ready to begin looking for a home?"

Austin brought up a housing search engine and put in his parameters. He could count on one hand the number of places he could afford. "Yep. Received pre-approval tonight." He told her the amount he was willing to spend and waited for her to tell him to take his business elsewhere.

"You've given me quite the challenge, especially during the holiday season, but you've also seen that I love a challenge."

"Yes, I have, but before I agree to work with you, I want to make sure that your commission from me will be worth your time."

She laughed. "I would much rather work with you than the

prima donnas with their million-dollar budgets."

He heard clicking, probably her manicured fingernails on a keyboard.

"What areas would you prefer to look in?"

"I work in Amery, so within thirty minutes of there. Give or take depending upon the property."

More clicking. "Do you prefer a house, condo, townhome?"

"I'm flexible but would probably prefer a townhome so I don't have to worry about yardwork and snow shoveling."

"Those will typically come with Home Owner's Association fees."

"Yes, I'm aware."

"Okay." She asked a few more questions, narrowing down her search parameters. "I have my eye on a few properties as we speak. How soon do you want to start your search?"

"Tomorrow night good?"

"Let me check my calendar."

Austin listened to more clicking.

"I'm open. Prepare to look at a few homes."

"Where do we meet?"

"I'll pick you up, if that's okay. I'll message you when I get a time."

"I'm looking forward to it."

"Yeah, me too."

He hit the phone button, ending the call, and realized he had a goofy smile on his face. Seriously, dude? You're going house hunting, not on a date!

But something inside him still smiled at the thought of spending the evening with the dynamic Dani Chamberlain. He hoped he wasn't setting himself up for a fall.

Dani set aside her phone, grinning. To say she had a crush on a school teacher wasn't an exaggeration. He was so different from guys she'd dated, not that they'd been bad, but money tinted people's perspectives, as Austin's financial position had changed her perspective. He helped her see life through a different-colored lens, and she liked what she saw. Too much, perhaps, but that didn't mean she wasn't going to enjoy their time together, even if it was just looking at homes.

Maybe he'd join her on her own house hunt.

Okay, now she was getting ahead of herself.

This was a business venture, and nothing more, which meant she better get to work. His budget was small, but the area he was looking in was north of Minneapolis and would be more budget friendly than an urban home. She'd show him townhomes, but she'd also stretch his imagination a bit and show him single-family dwellings. Oftentimes owners would be able to hire out yard work and snow removal for less than HOA fees, saving him money there.

For the next couple of hours, she searched, took notes, and then narrowed down her list to three homes for the following night. This would be more of a get-to-know-you evening as she would be observing his reactions, seeing what he liked and disliked, what he valued in a home, and what wasn't as important. After that, the hunt would become easier and would take up less of her time, making her commission, though small, stretch further.

*See, Mom, I can be practical!* She felt like running downstairs to prove that fact.

And now she had to begin the house search for herself. This

would be far more frustrating. She logged onto the system, put in her must-haves and her budget and a big zero homes came up. If she hadn't been such a spendthrift for the last two years, she'd actually have a sizable down payment, but she'd been as reckless with her money as she'd been with her activities.

She hated to admit that her mom had done the right thing in taking away her apartment, but maybe if she went downstairs and buttered her mom up for a bit, she'd relent and give back Dani's old place. Nah, Mom would see right through her. No, it would be better to grovel and admit her wrongs. Mom wouldn't expect that, right?

Or maybe first, she should behave as Austin did and say a prayer first. It had been a long time—years—since she'd opened her Bible, much less uttered a heartfelt, selfless prayer. But when God takes away your dad, He earns the silent treatment. God probably liked that just as much as her mom and uncle.

And it was just as childish when she gave God the silent treatment.

Once again, she found her mom in the basement in front of the television, but tonight she had her computer in front of her as well. Always working, whether at home or in Washington, which she'd be returning to tomorrow night, leaving Dani alone in this massive house. Seemed like such a waste.

"Hey, Mom." She sat alongside her, formulating her plan to ask for help with a down payment. "No chocolate tonight?"

She laughed. "The last time I had it, you ate it all."

"About that . . . " She set her laptop next to her mom's but didn't open it. "I've had quite the weekend."

Mom leaned over and closed her laptop. Preparing to listen? Huh. Maybe she'd had an eye-opening weekend as well.

"I served at that Family Table Meal, as you suggested. And

they even want me back."

"Good for you." She patted Dani's hand like she used to when Dani was a little girl.

"As long as I dress appropriately, that is, and leave my purse behind."

Mom tilted back her head and laughed. "I had the same lecture, but thankfully I received it before I went to the church, so I had time to change."

"You've served there?"

"Why do you think I made the recommendation?"

"But people were shocked that the"—she made air quotes—"senator's daughter would show up. And no one mentioned you."

"Sometimes I like to be anonymous, so I use my maiden name. And if people recognize me, they're gracious enough to not accuse me of being in politics."

"Makes sense. Felicity Olson sure beats Chamberlain. No one mistakes me. Maybe I should adopt that approach and go by Danielle Olson. It would be nice to be anonymous."

"Honey." Mom patted her hand again. "You're too much like your father. You command attention. Even if your name was Jane Doe, you would be noticed."

She sighed and sunk into the couch. "But maybe I've changed."

"In one weekend?"

She sat up and looked her mom directly in the eye. "I admit, I've been a spoiled brat." She shook her head. "On Sunday, I also went with a group to the tent city in Minneapolis."

"You did what?" Mom raised her voice and jerked straight up.

"Calm down, I was with a large group of people. We went in daylight and were safe." With the exception of her little jaunt which Mom would never learn about.

"You're going to be the death of me yet."

"I'm sorry. I wish I could change."

Mom laughed. "No, you don't. And I don't want you to change, even if it gives my heart a few extra jolts here and there. Probably good for my old ticker."

"You're not old. Fifty is the new thirty, right?"

"I'm fifty-five."

"Whatever. Point is, you're still young, but I met people this weekend, talked with people who were probably my age yet looked like they were seniors. They lived in unimaginable conditions and treated their bodies even worse, as if there's no hope for them at all. But then I also met amazing people who selflessly devote their time to helping even though they know not to expect immediate, if any, results. They just say they want to love on the people, so they see Jesus."

Mom drew in a deep breath and looked toward the TV, but her eyes weren't focused. "That's the thing about serving. You do it not to grab attention, but because it's the right thing to do, and yes, you do hope that those you're serving see Jesus. I do know that as a servant, I see Him all the time, and He's always teaching me."

"Is that why you're in politics?"

She shook her head. "When I started out, absolutely. Like any greenhorn, I was going to change the world." She raised her fist in the air. "But when you're in a position of power, the world changes you."

"Sounds like you have regrets."

"My biggest regret is not spending more time with you and your brother. And your father before he passed."

"That's mine too." She leaned against the back of the couch and curled her legs beneath her, when what she really wanted was to snuggle with her mother like she used to do with her father. "Do you think that's why he went down to that part of town that night? To gain attention?"

Mom's eyes took on a glazed look as she stared straight ahead. "Yes, your father craved attention, but he also had a heart for the poor, just as you do. If I'd kept him away from the bad parts of town, it would have smothered his spirit. Just as if I told you not to go, I'd smother you." She patted Dani's hand, which was as touchy-feely as her mom would get. "I love your passion for people, sweetheart. It keeps me grounded and reminds me why I went into politics in the first place. You just keep being who God made you to be, and I'll work on getting back to the woman He created me to be."

"Guess we're both works-in-progress."

"That we are." Mom picked up her laptop. "Unfortunately, I have other works-in-progress I need to attend to. Was there a specific reason you came down here?"

*To ask for a down payment*, flitted through Dani's head, but after this rare heart-to-heart, she didn't want to spoil the moment. "Just to spend time with you. Tell you I love you."

"I love you, too, dear."

"I'll let you get back at it." She picked up her laptop and headed to her room. She hadn't accomplished what she'd come down here to do, but that was okay. She'd groveled and opened up, and then Mom had too, and that was far more valuable than asking for help with a down payment.

## Chapter Six

*W*hat do you wear house hunting?

Austin stared into his tiny closet, and nothing felt adequate. Maybe the better question was, what should he wear when house hunting with Dani Chamberlain. It shouldn't make a difference, but it did. He shouldn't want to impress her, but he did, and that was about the dumbest thing he'd felt since being homeless.

All that should really matter tonight was that he found a home. He should have hired the guy Richard suggested. Then he wouldn't have wasted the last half hour worrying about what to wear. What kind of idiot does that?

He groaned and finally settled on a pair of new jeans and a button-down shirt. He finished getting dressed just as the doorbell rang. Was this good enough?

*Oh, get over it, Lang!*

He hurried to the door, opened it, and stood speechless. Her outfit was simple really. Red peacoat and black slacks with a reddish blouse. Her hair and makeup were also modest, but he was figuring out that nothing Dani Chamberlain did would come off as understated. Very professional, yet stunning.

And breath stealing.

"Mind if I come in?" Dani's voice broke into his musing.

"Oh, yes. Of course." Panicked, he checked the daybed. It was made, thank goodness. No dishes in the sink either because he'd been too nervous to eat.

She stepped inside and looked around. "Seeing where you live now and how you decorate—or in your case, how you don't decorate—helps me know what to look for."

He stuffed his hands into his front pockets. "I guess hanging pictures was never a priority."

"There's nothing wrong with that." She walked over to a round table at the end of his bed and picked up the picture of his "family." "I recognize this guy. Richard, right?"

"Yep."

"And the rest?"

He stood beside her and pointed out everyone. "Um, that's my sister, Brittany. She's in her second year of college down in Florida. That's Richard's wife, Sheila, and those two are their kids, Matthew and Susanna."

"Your family."

"That's them." Not counting his mom in prison. She hadn't been family since she first started using drugs back before he'd turned ten.

"You're fortunate."

"Yeah, I am." Far more fortunate than those who hadn't been rescued from the street. He hated talking about himself, so he grabbed his jacket off a hook by his door and slipped on his winter shoes. "Should we go?"

She laughed. "You don't have to be nervous. I've sold a lot of houses. I know what I'm doing."

"But I don't."

"Which is why you hired me." She opened the door.

He gestured to the steps. "After you." He should open the car door for her, too, but she was driving. What was the gentlemanly thing to do then? If only Richard were here to guide him. Guess it was time he grew up.

She unlocked the car as they were walking toward it, so he whipped around the vehicle and opened the door for her.

"Thank you," she said as she stepped into her vehicle. "I can honestly say no one's ever done that for me before."

He shrugged. "Just thought it was the right thing to do."

"You're sweet."

He felt his face heat, so he jogged around her car and got in, gathering his wits. What was the matter with him? One pretty girl smiles at him, and he goes all gaga? Sheesh!

"Here are the homes I've scheduled showings at." She handed him three sheets of paper with home pictures and descriptions.

He glanced through them while Dani drove. A townhome, a condo, and a single-family home. All three were priced about the same, and all appeared to be solid contenders, at least on paper. Richard had warned him that the realtor's job was to make every home sound and look like it was the best around, so don't fall for their spiel. Look at everything with a critical eye. Turn on faucets. Flush toilets. Check the furnace, the AC unit. Test the appliances included in the sale. Look for cracks in walls, floors, foundation.

With all that could go wrong, it was a wonder that anyone bought or sold a house.

They stopped at the condo first. It was newly renovated, and he could move in as soon as his financing went through. It had great amenities, including an indoor pool, a gym, and indoor parking, but he'd pay for those amenities with a HOA fee that was higher than his mortgage payment would be per month. He checked that off the list immediately. He might as well be renting.

The single-family home was fifty years old, the original owners still lived there, and they hadn't updated it since it was built, but that was all cosmetic. The house was structurally sound. It came with a detached garage, and a privacy fence wrapped around the yard. If he wanted, he could get a dog. The one big negative was that it would take him forty-five minutes to get to work, and he had no desire to spend ninety minutes a day in the car.

He crossed that one off the list and hoped the townhome would be a match.

Distance-wise, it would only take him twenty-five minutes to get to work. Not great, but doable. The interior had been updated in the nineties, which was okay. Cosmetic stuff he could deal with. What he didn't like were the thin walls he could hear the neighbors through. Another no-go.

After getting the car door for Dani, he got in, buckled, and slumped in the seat. Tonight hadn't gone at all as he'd hoped.

"Well that was a productive evening." She started her car and pulled out of the townhome's parking space.

"Productive? How? Everything was a no."

"Right. But look at what we learned tonight. You don't mind dealing with cosmetic changes. A single-family home is definitely an option." She shot him a smile. "You'd like to have a dog."

"And I don't like high HOAs, thin walls, or long commutes."

"Exactly. So that helps me tremendously in your home search. It will tighten the parameters I search with, so we spend less time on the road, and the homes we'll actually look at should be solid contenders."

"Okay, so when do we go out next? I'm free every night this week."

Dani flicked on her blinker. "I don't know my schedule offhand, but we'll find a night that works, and I'll find you a place you can call home."

*Home.*

He liked the sound of that. A place he could call his own, and maybe put up a wall hanging or two. A place he wouldn't mind showing off to the right woman, maybe cook her a meal. But he'd never know if a woman was the right one if he didn't ask anyone out. Now was as good time as any to begin.

"So," came out in soprano. He cleared his throat. "Uh, since it's still early, could I treat you to dinner? I haven't eaten yet, and there's this little hole-in-the-wall place near me that serves the best burgers." Really, Austin? Burgers? For all he knew, she was a vegan.

"Oh, I love burgers! Show me the way."

Whew. A woman who liked a good burger. Definitely a plus.

He gave directions to the café, and within twenty minutes they were seated and had ordered.

And he was completely out of words. He sat across from her, fiddling with his silverware, chastising himself for the impulsive gesture while she sat as silently as he. What made him think he, the formerly homeless kid, son of a convict, should ask out a beautiful and popular daughter of a senator? She was basically an American princess. And him? In comparison, he was a pauper.

*Say something, dude. Don't sit there looking like the idiot you are.*

"So, hey, I'm sorry I was so picky tonight." Brilliant, dude, just brilliant.

Her eyes brightened. Maybe it wasn't such a stupid statement after all.

"Picky? You thought you were picky?"

"I didn't like any of the homes you showed me. After looking online and at your sheets, I thought I'd want them all."

"That's because we realtors only show their beauty marks not their warts. Besides, did you once complain about popcorn ceilings?"

"Huh?"

"The bumpy, textured ceiling that almost look like popped corn."

"Oh. People don't like that?"

She rolled her eyes. "You'd think it was the worst housing design ever. And not once did you complain about no quartz countertops or stainless-steel appliances or no master bath."

"Didn't know I was supposed to."

"Well, you obviously don't watch that channel with all the renovations and house hunting. It's completely spoiled people. No one looks at the bones of a house anymore, they just see the cosmetics, so you were a joy to work with tonight."

"Whew. That's good to know. I'll go home tonight and catch up on all those shows so I know how to properly complain next time."

"Uh-uh. I'm going to steal your remote, so you can't access them."

"You'll have to steal my computer too."

"If I have to."

They both laughed, taking away the awkward tension.

Austin took a sip of water. "So, tell me more about you. I don't pay attention to political gossip."

"You don't know how grateful I am for that. Every time I go on a date, the guy already knows way more about me than I know about him, and it's all the salacious stuff. I'm really not a bad person, but the press says otherwise."

"Then let me tell you what I know about you. You've got a big heart, amazing passion. The way you took off without thinking when someone needed help yesterday blew me away."

She laughed. "Is that why you lectured me?"

"No. I lectured you because you scared me to death."

"And I broke the rules."

"That too."

"I'm sorry for that. I'm impulsive. Guess I take after my dad."

"Tell me about him."

Her eyes lit up. "He was artistic and passionate and had the biggest heart. Since Mom was an attorney and then got into politics, he stayed at home with me and Brad."

"Your brother?"

"Yeah, older brother. He became a pastor. Lives down in Missouri where people don't care about Felicity Chamberlain. He credits Dad staying home with us, while Mom worked, for his going into the ministry."

"Were you homeschooled?'

"Oh, absolutely not. Dad would have, but Mom insisted we go to public school. As a public schooling advocate, she didn't want her constituents seeing a hypocrite."

"If you don't mind my asking, what happened to your dad?"

Her gaze clouded over, and she stared toward the window showcasing fresh fallen snow.

Shoot, he should have kept his mouth shut. "I'm sorry. If you don't want to talk about it, I completely understand."

"No." She looked back at him and offered a sad smile. "Most people know the story. Dad was killed while helping people at a homeless encampment. He died doing what he loved."

"Oh man, I'm sorry. I didn't mean to—"

She held up her hand. "Really, talking about him isn't a problem, but you'd think my heart wouldn't still break after fifteen years."

"Breakfast Patty Special." Their server seemed to materialize out of nowhere and set Austin's plate heaped with a burger and tater tots in front of him, "And the Peanut Butter Patty" in front of Dani.

Dani's face brightened up. "Perfect timing, wouldn't you say?"

Yep. Perfect. That conversation was far too deep for a realtor/client relationship. Instead he pointed a finger at her burger and wrinkled his nose. "Peanut butter on a hamburger? That's not right."

"Oh, but it's so good!" She cut her sandwich in half and took a bite. Her eyes closed, and she moaned. "You should try it sometime."

"I'll stick with my breakfast burger." He picked up his sandwich that had egg yolk dripping off the side of the burger and took a bite. Beyond delicious every time. And the tater tots were equally delectable. If he ate like this all the time, he could roll all the way home.

"This is a dangerous place." Dani dipped a tot into ketchup.

"Tell me about it." Hopefully that would be a safer subject than talking about her dad. Austin took another bite which was even better than the first. Interesting how good food tasted when you were hungry. But back when he was homeless, he never savored the food he ate—it was a means to stay alive.

"Now it's your turn." Dani set her sandwich on the plate. "What makes you tick? Why are you so passionate about working with the homeless?"

He set down his burger. Guess there was no avoiding a deep conversation, but how much should he tell her? Not that he was ashamed—he'd told his story countless times—but somehow with Dani it felt more personal as if it would alter their relationship. Why that mattered, he didn't know.

"If you don't want to talk about it, I get it." She reached across the table and touched his hand. "We'll postpone the discussion for now."

"No. That's not it, I just . . . " He puffed out a breath, trying to come up with the right words. "The diners at the Family Table Meal? Those people at the homeless camp? That used to be me."

"You?" Dani blinked, as if trying to process what he was saying. "You were homeless?"

He laughed, but definitely not out of humor. People were always shocked when they learned, but his story also gave others hope. "I aged out of foster care and lived in the broken-down car my mom had given me. The one I still drive today. I used to eat at that Family Table Meal. Richard and his wife rescued me, and now, five years later, here I am." He opened his palms and spread his arms.

"Oh, my goodness." Her head seemed to be on a continuous swivel. "So that explains your unique family."

"Yep." He grinned. "And now my younger sister—my blood relative—is going to college in Florida. Wants to be a social worker."

"Good for her."

"Right? I'm super-proud of her. In high school, she had a good social worker, so now she wants to help others as she was helped."

"Just like you."

He shrugged. "Yeah, I guess so."

"But why were you homeless? Where was your mom? Your dad?"

"Mom"—he made air quotes—"was the type of person you saw this past weekend. She was into drugs, booze, prostitution. When I was fifteen, she went to prison, and it was a relief. I ended up homeless but didn't have to deal with her craziness anymore. As for my father, he's some sperm donor somewhere in the world."

"I'm so sorry. I ... I can't imagine." Tears glistened like twinkle lights in Dani's eyes. "I will never, ever complain about my upbringing again." She pulled a tissue from her purse and wiped her eyes. "What you must have—"

Her phone played some song. "Rats." She dug into her purse. "I'm sorry, I have to take this. It's my brother, and he never calls." She retrieved her phone and swiped to answer. "Hey, Brad, nice timing." She rolled her eyes at Austin then grinned. "I'm sitting here with a good-looking guy—" The grin slid from her face as her brother talked, and she dabbed the tissue at her eyes. "They called you first? ... Oh, pastor privilege." She snorted. "Of course. I'm heading there right now." She threw her phone into her purse and stood, bumping the table and knocking over her water glass. "Oh, I'm sorry." She started drying it with a napkin.

He took the napkin from her. "I've got this. What's wrong?"

"It's my mother." She wiped the back of her hand over her cheeks. "She had a heart attack and is in the hospital. I've got to go."

She fumbled in her purse and pulled out her keys which fell to the floor. "I'm sorry. I'm a mess."

"I've got this." He hurried around the table and picked up her keys. "I'll drive."

"But—"

"No buts." He waved over the server, handed him a couple of twenties, then left the restaurant with Dani, praying her mother would be okay.

## Chapter Seven

*D*ani sat in the passenger seat, hugging herself, numb. Just when things were getting better with her mom. She sniffled and plucked a tissue from the center console.

Looking upward, she hurled angry thoughts. *You better not take her, God. You already have my dad. Isn't that enough?*

Like always, God, *if* He even existed, was giving her the silent treatment. Maybe that was who she'd learned it from.

"How are you doing?" Austin flicked on the blinker and turned into the hospital parking lot.

"How do you think I'm doing?" She wiped her nose and shook her head. Austin didn't deserve that. "I'm sorry. I'm scared. Angry. What if Mom doesn't make it?"

"I don't know. Whatever happens, I'll be here for you."

How could he make that promise when they barely knew each other? It was a promise she wouldn't hold him to.

He drove up to the emergency entrance. "Go on in. I'll park."

"No, just take me to the ramp. I don't want you to see the circus."

"And you shouldn't face that circus alone."

"I won't be alone, I'll have . . . " Who? Uncle Harris and Aunt Helen would be here, but Brad wouldn't arrive for several hours.

Her girlfriends were as shallow as she was and would be no support at all. Work relationships were meant to stay at work. Her activist friends were probably all protesting at the capital. Many of them liked to protest just because. She needed a reason. Usually. And Mom's cronies would only be concerned with how her heart attack affected them and why she wasn't in Washington this week for the "important" vote. Mom's life was far more important, thank you!

Then there was the press who would be in Dani's face, probably blaming her because of her arrest.

They weren't the only ones. Austin shouldn't see that side of her.

She gestured toward the parking ramp. "Please. I can't subject you to them."

"That isn't your decision. Now get out and go to your mother."

She opened her door and looked back at him. "Anyone ever tell you you're bossy?"

He shrugged. "I'll be right there."

Without another word, she closed the car door and rushed through the revolving doors into the hospital. No surprise, she was immediately accosted by TV cameras and reporters shoving microphones into her face.

"How is your mother doing?"

"Do you think your recent escapades had anything to do with your mother's health?"

Oh, how she wished she could tell those reporters where they could stuff their mics, but that would certainly make the headlines. A few days ago, she wouldn't have cared, but this short time spent with people who had real problems had already mellowed her. Life wasn't just about her.

Instead of verbally responding to the press, she pushed

through them and hurried up to the coronary care unit, but not without being waylaid by more supposed journalists. Didn't they have anything better to do than harass the grieving?

She found her aunt and uncle in the waiting room where no press was allowed, thank goodness. "How is she? Have you heard anything else?" She tossed the questions toward her aunt and uncle as she breezed through the waiting room on the way to her mom's room.

Uncle Harris leapt up and walked alongside her. "She's stable. They're running tests, giving her a bunch of drugs."

"Oh, I bet she loves that."

"She fought against every one." Uncle Harris cupped a hand on her shoulder, slowing her down. "Dani, she's not in her room. I said, they're running tests."

"Oh." She stopped and shook her head. "I'm sorry, I heard you, but I didn't process. I just want to see her. I want her to know that I'm here for her, that I love her."

"She knows that, sweetheart." He looped an arm over her shoulders and led her back to the waiting room.

She sat, elbows on her knees and face in her hands. "It's my fault," she muttered.

"Danielle Chamberlain." Aunt Helen pulled down Dani's hands. "We will not have any of that talk. Your mother's heart's been bad for years."

"And my antics made it worse."

"Making this all about you won't make her any better, so stop feeling sorry for yourself. Your mother loves you just as you are and frankly, you keep her young." Her aunt dug knitting out of a handbag. "Now sit up straight. You don't want to grow old with a hunched back, do you?"

"Yes, ma'am." A smile almost slipped out as her aunt's

knitting needles clanked together.

"Dani?"

She looked up at Austin, and a smile did break free. For all her talk about wanting him to go home, she was very glad he stayed.

"And who is this?" Her aunt's needles stopped moving. "You look familiar, young man."

"Aunt Helen, Uncle Harris, this is Austin Lang. He's the director of the Family Table Meal."

"Ah, that's it." Uncle Harris stood and shook Austin's hand.

"You're Dani's uncle." Austin looked down the hallway that led to her mother's room. "So, your sister . . . " He glanced at Dani and smiled. "Is your mom. I never realized she was the senator. I just thought the two of you were average volunteers."

"Well, we probably don't live up to average, but we do like to help out at your meal. It's a fine service you're offering the community."

"It's not my doing, I just happen to organize it most Saturdays. That's the easy part. The volunteers work a lot harder than I do."

"Son, you'd make a fine politician."

Austin chuckled. "Thanks, but no thanks. I'll stick to teaching."

"And a teacher, too." Aunt Helen nudged Dani in the shoulder. "Looks like you have a fine catch."

"But we're not dating." Dani looked up at Austin, her eyes wide. Did she see a flicker of disappointment?

"What she said. Dani's my realtor. We were out looking at houses."

"Well, that's a shame." Aunt Helen resumed her knitting. "You'd be good for her, young man."

"We're friends, and you never know where that might lead." Austin winked at Dani as he pulled her keys out of his pocket. He held them in mid-air. "So, your mom, how is she doing?"

"They're running tests, is all we know." Dani took her keys from Austin. "But I do know that I'll be worthless to you this week." She pulled out a business card from her purse. "Gavin's the best in our office. Besides me, of course."

He accepted the card but looked at it with his mouth twisted. "I can wait until you're ready."

"That would be fine if you had more than a month to find a home. You can't wait for me. Trust me, you're in good hands with Gavin."

"Fine. I'll give him a call." He stuck the card into his front pocket. "And let me know about Saturday? If you're not up to it, I get it."

"Sure thing." Dani got up. "I'll walk you out."

"And face the vultures?"

"That's right." Understanding his need to leave, but not wanting him to go, she grasped his hand and led him a few feet down the hall. There, she spoke barely above a whisper, not wanting her aunt and uncle to hear. "Thanks for everything tonight. Can you get home okay?"

"I'll call an Uber. No problem."

Keeping his hand in hers, she stepped closer, gnawing on her lower lip. "Think I can get a raincheck on dinner?"

He took a step back. "When your mom's feeling better, you bet."

"You're the best." She stood on her tippy-toes and pressed a kiss to his cheek.

His face turned an adorable shade of pink, which he must have realized because he looked down. "I try. Keep me posted, okay?" He didn't wait for an answer but pulled his hand from hers and hurried down the hall toward the elevator.

She moaned and hid her face in her hands. She'd done it again. Let her haywire emotions get the best of her, flirting with Austin at this highly inappropriate time. He was going to think her a total flake.

He'd be thinking the truth.

She shuffled down the hallway back to her aunt and uncle as a woman in scrubs strode their way. Uncle Harris and Aunt Helen bounced from their chairs and Dani hurried to her uncle's side.

"Dr. Hansen, this is Danielle Chamberlain, my sister's daughter. How is she doing?"

"Nice to meet you, Ms. Chamberlain. Your mother's arteries are severely clogged, so we're recommending an angioplasty."

Dani blinked, trying to process what Dr. Hansen had said. "You mean, right now?"

"As soon as we can get her into the operating room. The hope is that this will prevent the need for open-heart surgery in the future, which is far more invasive and requires much more recovery time."

"Is it dangerous, the angioplasty?"

"There are always risks." The doctor listed them off, including blood clots, arrhythmia, damage to blood vessels, another heart attack.

Dani swallowed. This was her mother's life they were talking about, and none of the options were good.

"Do what you have to do."

The doctor hurried away, and Dani plopped down in her chair to do the only thing she could think of.

Pray.

So that was what it must be like to be caught up in a tornado. Austin flopped down on his daybed, not bothering to pull back the covers, and closed his eyes. Since he'd met Dani, his life had been a whirlwind. She was going to wear him out.

He rubbed a hand on his cheek where it still tingled from her light kiss and grinned.

Being worn out by Tornado Dani might not be such a bad thing. Oh man, he was a goner. He'd call Richard, but then he'd be lectured on how stupid following your heart was and that there was no such thing as love at first sight, blah, blah, blah. But you couldn't be indifferent to Danielle Chamberlain. That was impossible.

Yet, he'd just met her.

On top of that, her mom was in the hospital. The last thing she'd be thinking about was a hick like him.

And the first thing he should do is pray for Dani, her mom, and her family.

He pounded his pillow, hoping to drive some sense into his brain. It had to be adrenaline. He'd spend the next hour in prayer, then by tomorrow morning his brain and his heart would be back to normal. And by the time Saturday came, this asinine crush would be gone.

# Chapter Eight

Austin massaged a headache as he entered his apartment Tuesday evening. The kids must have known he wasn't on his A game today, because they pushed every button he had until he felt like exploding. He'd take his frustrations out on the stovetop tonight by cooking some comfort food, hamburger hot dish, just the way his grandma had taught him.

He could correct papers while watching an Indiana Jones movie. Those always took him away from the present and helped him relax.

Tomorrow he'd give this Gavin from Dani's realty office a call and get things set up with him. As much as he wanted to stick with Dani, he couldn't wait for her to return to work.

He started browning hamburger and his cell phone rang from some unknown number. Then it dinged that he had a message. While stirring the meat, he listened:

"Hey Austin, this is Gavin Schultz from Star Realty. Dani gave me your info and asked me to call. I've found some homes that fit exactly what you're looking for and am available for showings tonight yet but will be busy then through Saturday afternoon. Give me a call, and we'll see what we can set up. Look forward to working with you."

Tonight?

Or Saturday.

Time was too short as it was. He couldn't chance waiting, so he turned off the burner and gave Gavin a call. Five minutes later, Gavin had three showings scheduled. The man certainly was a go-getter. Any other night, Austin would appreciate it.

He stored the hamburger in the fridge then made a simple peanut butter and strawberry jelly sandwich. Bea's homemade jelly was the best he'd ever had. Maybe before he moved, she'd finally give him the recipe.

Gavin showed up before Austin had his sandwich eaten, so he stuffed it in his mouth as Gavin jogged down the steps to his Mercedes. At least Austin would be riding in style.

"You'll love riding in this baby." Gavin ran his hand over the dashboard. "She purrs like a lion."

"Nice." Austin tried putting emotion into his response, but he couldn't care less about this car. All he cared was that it got them from point A to point B.

"What do you drive?" Gavin pulled onto the road and jackrabbited toward the stoplight in spite of the ice-coated roads.

Austin reached up for the handle above the window. "A Honda Civic."

"They always run, don't they?"

Sort of like Gavin's mouth. He didn't shut up during the entire drive to the first house, a Tudor surrounded by neighbors who didn't know what a trash can was. Then they checked out a 1950s rambler that was the perfect size and a terrific price, but the roof and windows needed to be replaced right away. Given the low price, it was still an option. Then the final home they toured was an end-unit townhome. Single-car garage. Two-bedrooms, one and a half baths. That was all he needed. Plus, it had a fireplace. That was a bonus. This could be the one.

He got into Gavin's car and tuned the man out. The dude must love hearing himself talk. Now if Austin was with Dani, he'd complain about the popcorn ceilings, the white appliances, faux wood countertops, and linoleum kitchen floor just to get a rise out of her. He had mentioned the carpeted bathroom to Gavin. What possessed people to put carpet on their bathroom floor?

Maybe he should call her and complain. That would get a laugh and brighten his day. He needed to call her anyway to see how she was doing and ask how her mom was, beyond what the press was reporting. Or maybe Gavin had more info, after all he'd known Dani a lot longer than Austin had.

Austin butted right into one of Gavin's monologues about the best foreign cars. "What have you heard about Senator Chamberlain?"

"You do speak. Dani said you're a quiet one which is dangerous around me because, as you've heard, I like to talk. But anyway, the scuttlebutt I hear about the senator is that she had an angioplasty and should be released from the hospital in a day or two and in week or so she should be able to return to Washington."

"Thanks for the update." Which wasn't any more detailed than the news accounts. So, did that mean Dani would be able to help on Saturday? He hoped so, which said a lot about his feelings for her.

Man, it had been one crazy week. Dani slipped on her jogging pants and shoes, desperately needing to get away from this house. Her mom had turned into a whiny baby and Brad had returned home this morning. All Dani had done all week was run errands for her mom. Even if the errands were just around home, this house was so huge that she got in a workout going up and down the stairs. What she needed was fresh air—albeit, winter air—and a friendly voice.

She grabbed her cell phone and stopped in the office to let her mom know she was going for a run. Then she donned her winter coat and gloves and escaped out the front door.

Free at last!

The air froze her lungs as she jogged down to the Mississippi then ran along the path her mom had had paved some time back when she used to run. The groundskeepers were diligent about keeping the path free from snow in the winter, even if the path went unused. If Mom wanted her heart to keep beating, she better start running again.

Dani reached a gazebo about a half mile away from the house and sat on a bench to take in the view and the silence.

In the past, after an emotional week, she'd go protest at an abortion clinic to chase away her anxiety. That was one protest her mom never complained about.

But now . . .

Amazing how one weekend transformed her way of thinking. Yes, a week ago she'd brought attention to those who lived in the tent city, but on Saturday and Sunday, she'd actually done something about it rather than wagging her finger at others for ignoring the situation. Oh, she'd become an excellent finger wagger.

For once, she'd taken real action, and it felt good, like she was doing something worthwhile.

Tomorrow, she'd get to volunteer at the Family Table Meal again, and she couldn't wait! Working alongside others, she'd seen there wasn't a lack of action, but rather people preferred not to advertise their good deeds.

Like her mom and her uncle.

Why did she not know that they served at the Family Table Meal? If the public knew that side of her mom, she'd have no trouble getting re-elected. Oh, Dani knew the Bible verse about not letting your left hand know what your right hand was doing and to let your giving be a secret, but that made no sense to her.

She looked up at the sky just beginning to fade along with the sunset. "I don't get it, God. Your followers are out there working and giving and being so secretive about it that the world doesn't have a clue. How does that help your kingdom? All they see and hear are the extremes who don't represent You. Just think of what my mom could accomplish if her constituents knew about the charities she supported. They'd know Mom cares and that she isn't just another power-hungry politician."

No surprise, God gave her the silent treatment.

Hopefully, Austin wouldn't. Maybe he'd have an answer. Her mom had kept her so busy, she hadn't spoken with him since Monday. Austin would understand her silence, wouldn't he? He was a guy, and they didn't worry about stuff like that.

Did they?

She stretched her legs out on the bench and dialed Austin's number. Hummingbirds took flight in her stomach at the mere thought of hearing his voice. She'd dated a lot in her young life, but Austin was by far the most genuine person she'd met. Showed she didn't get outside her bubble very often.

The phone rang a number of times and then voice mail picked up. He didn't even have a personalized message that allowed her to hear his voice, but she left a message for him. "Hey, it's Dani. Hope you're doing okay. I plan to come tomorrow morning—I've thought of little else all week. I love what you're doing there.

Anyway, that's not why I called. I'd like to get together. I have questions for you. Oh, I suppose I could ask my brother, but—"

The voice mail cut off. Austin would probably be thrilled to hear from her as he'd had the joy of spending an evening with garrulous Gavin. The man knew his real estate, but he never shut up.

*I wonder if they found something on Tuesday . . .* Gavin hadn't said. One more reason to talk with Austin.

She looked at her phone again. She could call Brad with her Bible question, after all, he did have an MDiv. But when he talked religion, he tended to put her to sleep. Maybe because she learned more from action than speeches. Austin wouldn't just recite from some text book or spout Bible verses, he'd show her.

Tomorrow at the meal, she planned to watch and learn.

Austin stepped out of the shower, refreshed. This teaching career was going to be more exhausting than he'd anticipated, but he loved it. He loved watching the faces of his students when a concept clicked. This unit on home finances came at the perfect time as he used his home hunting experience as an example.

Now all he needed was to cap off the week with a call to Dani, tell her he thought he'd found his home. Hopefully he'd see her tomorrow.

After putting on pajama bottoms, he took his phone and the daily mail to his daybed. He grinned when he saw that Dani had called and left a message. His grin grew when he listened to the message. Yay for her coming tomorrow! She had spiritual questions maybe? Why wouldn't she ask her brother? He hit quick dial while going through his mail. Junk. Junk. More junk.

A letter.

He stopped breathing and stared at the return address.

*Audra Lang*
*Minnesota Correctional Facility*
*Sheridan, Minnesota 56004*

A letter from his mom in prison. She hadn't written him once in her seven years there. She'd even removed his name from the approved visitor list.

What could she possibly want?

"Hey Austin."

He startled at the sound of Dani's voice. "Uh, hi." With his finger, he slit open the envelope.

"Are you there? You called me."

He shook the cobwebs from his brain. "Uh, yeah, I'm here, it's just that I received a letter from my mom. She's never written. Ever." And he didn't know if he wanted to read what she had to say.

"What did she say?"

"I . . . I don't know." His voice shook. "I haven't read it yet."

"Would you like to read it to me? Or we can hang up and you can call back once you've read it."

"Yeah, let's do that." He tapped the end call button while half in a stupor. He pulled a single, folded sheet of paper from the envelope and it took two seconds to read, igniting a firestorm in his gut.

He hit redial and a ring later, Dani answered. "Are you okay?"

He laughed, but the situation was far from humorous. "Looks like I'm going to have a housemate when I move. My mom's getting out of prison on March first, and she said she's coming to live with me."

## Chapter Nine

*A*ustin scooped the burger with a spatula and slapped it on the griddle. Grease splattered, stinging his arm. Schnot! He flailed his arm and licked at the burning grease, thankful that the volunteer noise level in the church's kitchen covered his frustration.

"You know." Dani spoke just above a whisper behind him. "I'm not a cook, but generally if you turn the burgers gently, they don't fight back."

He turned and gave her the stink eye.

But she just grinned. "Someone didn't sleep well."

"Someone didn't sleep at all." He shook his head, trying to break up the one-way track in his mind. He'd spent all night on the computer, researching how to prepare for a parent's release from prison. There were lots of articles about spouses, particularly husbands, getting out of prison. And even more articles on parents coming home to small children, but how was the adult child supposed to handle it?

He flipped several more burgers, this time doing as Dani suggested.

"Good job." She patted his back.

"Don't you have something better to do?" He growled.

"Oh, there's a guest now." She whispered in his ear. "After

this, I'm taking you out and you can vent to me." She hurried away, hopefully to greet guests.

Could he vent to Dani? About the messed-up house hunt, a home that would now include his mom.

*Save money* was at the top of to-do lists for those expecting loved ones home from prison. The person being released would likely have difficulty finding a job, so they'd need financial support. Currently, his savings were going toward his down payment, and he was just beginning to have money for a few extras. No way did he have the funds to support another adult.

*Get them involved in church or the community. Have them see a counselor.* As if he'd have any control over his mother. Ha!

He wanted to tell her *no way*. She hadn't been a mother to him, so why should he be a son to her?

Because of that little commandment that said, "Honor your father and mother." It was not a conditional commandment, telling him to honor her *if* she was honorable. Besides, how could he, an advocate for the homeless, put his own mother on the streets?

Grrr.

He stared down at the burgers becoming too done on the griddle. *Get your head in the game, Lang.* Playing with fire wasn't the smartest thing to do when distracted. Maybe he should stand at the food assembly bar instead. He could slap lettuce and tomatoes on a bun without hurting anyone.

No, he could do this. Just banish his mom to the farthest corners of his mind until the meal was over.

He flipped the burgers again, then added the fully cooked ones to a platter and brought that over to the plate assembly table. There, volunteers topped the lettuce- and tomato-covered bun with a burger, then added tater tots and a fruit bowl to the plate before servers delivered the meal to their guests. Other servers went around the dining hall, filling cups with coffee and glasses with milk or juice.

He glanced out at the room filled with homeless people, some inhaling the only decent meal they'd had all week, others savoring it. He'd been one of the inhalers who never got full.

If he didn't take his mother in, would he see her here?

"I'm burnt!" Someone screamed. "I'm burnt!"

Austin ran out of the kitchen and saw that the diner was already being attended to.

Someone whirred past him, dropping dirty dishes in a container full of the same, then aimed for the screamer.

Dani. Why wasn't he surprised?

He caught up to her and grabbed her arm. "Let it be. She's taken care of."

"But she's hurt." She wriggled away from him.

"I said, don't." He used his scolding teacher voice, which stopped Dani.

She glared back at him. "I am not a child."

*Then don't act like one*, he wanted to blurt out, but thankfully that stuck in his throat. He tightened his fists, sending all his negative energy there, and put on his teacher hat. "That's Clarice. She's always complaining about someone spilling on her, which is the reason why our coffee is only lukewarm and wouldn't hurt a baby's skin. And that guy helping her? He's a paramedic by trade, so he's got it under control. You and I would just get in the way."

"So, I'm supposed to stand here, helpless?"

"Not helpless. Staying out of the way is helping. Someone else has already cleaned up the mess, another person's calming Clarice. People hovering would further agitate her."

"Oh." Dani shoulders slumped, then she looked up at him and grinned. "Got your mind off of other things, didn't I?"

He opened his mouth and immediately closed it.

"The people are hungry." She poked him in the chest. "You better get in the kitchen and fry some burgers, Mister Meal Organizer Man." Still grinning, she spun on her heel and returned to serving.

And he stood there, his mouth agape.

"That spitfire's caught-cher eye, ain't she?" A man with a filthy, too-large coat and whiskers coated with dirt handed Austin an empty glass.

Austin stared at the glass then out at Dani flitting from one guest to the next. He'd never seen someone who could make these people smile so big. She was seeing them, every person, and making each feel important.

So, yeah, she'd caught his eye all right, just like she'd snagged the attention of everyone in the room.

The real question was, had he caught hers?

Taking a small break, Dani wiped the perspiration from her forehead and shot a glance into the kitchen. Austin was still there at the stove, scrubbing it clean. And he wasn't doing it out of obligation or for assigned community service or for accolades or to impress anyone. Having grown up in a political family, she didn't know that was possible.

Now that was real love.

And it was very attractive. But the guy was wound tighter than a brand-new yo-yo, not that she blamed him after receiving that letter from his mom.

By the end of the day, she planned to eradicate that tension. In the meantime, she had to spend a few minutes with her BFF-to-be, Sammi, who, no surprise, was seated in the back corner by herself.

Last week Sammi had gobbled down that chocolate cake. Maybe sweets would be a good icebreaker for today.

Dani perused the tableful of treats donated by a local bakery. No chocolate cake, but there were brownies and vanilla cupcakes and donuts and fritters. She plated one of each and brought them to her someday friend. This time she didn't ask permission to sit.

"Hey, Sammi." She set the plate in the middle of the table, between them. "Have a preference?"

The woman grabbed the brownie without looking up at Dani.

*So, she prefers chocolate.* Smart woman.

Dani took the fritter and broke it in half before taking a bite. Not bad. Wasn't chocolate, but it was definitely edible.

Now the question was, how do you begin a conversation with someone who was homeless and likely jobless? The usual icebreakers or small talk would simply not work.

"How was your burger?"

The woman shrugged. "Edible."

Progress.

"Well, I loved mine." Which she had.

The woman shoved the remainder of her brownie into her mouth, probably hoping to send a leave-me-alone message.

Dani received it, all right, but chose to ignore it. "Is there anything else I can get for you?"

"Yeah. Get the"—the woman cursed— "out of my space."

Good thing Dani was used to hearing people curse at her—mostly because of who her mother was—or she'd become discouraged. That wasn't happening.

"Then I'll see you next week, Sammi." She reached for the desserts, but the woman snatched them from Dani's hand.

Dani just put on a smile. "Enjoy." Then she left the table. Whew, this Sammi was a challenge. Dani loved a challenge.

Her gaze flitted to Austin, who still scrubbed the stove. Did the man ever relax? Or have fun?

Challenge accepted.

She strode past the mostly-cleaned tables into the kitchen and grabbed the dishrag out of Austin's hands. "You should go sit."

He grabbed the dishrag back. "As soon as I'm done with the stove."

She reached for the rag again,

But he held it away. "Uh-uh."

"Fine. But then you're going to put it down and relax. Maybe write a letter to your mom."

"I'd have nothing nice to say."

"Is that a problem? You should be honest. It would be good for your mental health."

"Ha!" He dipped the rag into sudsy water.

"Okay, then you should go have some fun."

He snorted. "Fun? What I need to do is find a house big enough for me and my mom." He scrubbed at non-existent dirt on the stove.

"And we'll find one for you. Gavin said you liked a townhouse?"

"Only two bedrooms. That leaves no room for my sister to stay when she visits."

"Okay. So, you want to look at three bedrooms instead. No problem. Or maybe a two-bedroom plus a loft?"

"Sure. Whatever."

"On it. But first you need to have fun."

He stopped scrubbing and squinted at her. "What is with you and *fun*?"

"I tend to enjoy it. I think you would too, if you gave it a try."

"I have fun."

"Sure, you do. When was the last time you did something that wasn't for anyone else?" She was reaching with this question—for all she knew, he partied every night—but the vibe he gave off didn't read that way.

"Doing things for others is fun."

She shook her head. He was a worse nut to crack than Sammi. "Okay. When is the last time you did something completely selfish?"

"I like video games."

She faked a yawn and covered her mouth. "Puhlease. When's the last time you did something fun with someone else? And don't say you played video games with Richard. Doesn't count."

"I don't know." He shrugged and threw his dishrag into a basket full of dirty linens. "Actually, yes, I do. I spent Thanksgiving with Richard's family."

"That's family." She shook her head. "Doesn't count."

"Doesn't anything count with you?"

"The right things do." She shrugged. "Before we do any more house hunting, you're coming with me to do something completely selfish, and we're going to have fun."

"So, we're going to watch a ball game? The Timberwolves are on tonight."

"Boring!" She rolled her eyes as the perfect idea came to her. "I have something much better in mind. I promise you'll have fun, and then we can dive into the house hunt. Deal?"

"If I don't have fun?"

She grinned. "With me, that's not a possibility."

## Chapter Ten

*A*ustin watched out the car window as they left the city behind, then the suburbs. They kept going on county roads until all that surrounded them were snow-covered fields and snow-flocked pines. Dani had made him grab his warmest gloves and his boots for this "fun" they were supposed to have, but to Austin fun wasn't something you had outside in the winter.

Being homeless in December had taught him well. "Where are we going?" He asked as Dani turned onto an ice-coated gravel road framed in by pine trees.

She threw a grin his way. "You'll see in a moment."

The trees seemed to pull aside and a massive hill that had a half-dozen children on sleds loomed in front of them.

"Ta-da!" She spread an arm Vanna-like toward the hill as if it was a giant scoop of ice cream.

About ice cream, he'd get excited.

She pulled off the road and parked on a makeshift lot occupied only by two pickups. "What do you think?"

He wrinkled his nose. "Yippee?"

"Oh, come on. Please tell me you like sledding."

"My grandma taught me not to lie." On the other hand, his mom had taught him the secret to getting away with lying.

"Huh. Well, by the end of the afternoon, I guarantee you'll have had a day to remember."

"Oh, you mean one spent in the emergency room with broken limbs?"

"Wow, you really don't know how to have fun." Dani shook her head and got out of the car.

She was right. When was the last time he'd let go of his responsibilities and just enjoyed himself? Sure, he'd spent time with the Brooks family, and that was always fun, but he couldn't recall the last time he'd gone out with friends. If he couldn't remember, that meant he was way overdue.

He got out of the Dani's car and joined her at the trunk where she'd stashed a couple of plastic toboggans. "Do you keep these in your car all the time?"

"I never know when I might have the need for escape." She removed a red sled.

He pulled out a blue one. "And playing in the cold is escape?"

"Out here, it is." She nodded to the hill. "It's nowhere near as crowded as the city hills plus they've got great hot cocoa."

"Well, if they have great hot cocoa . . . " He grinned and walked alongside her toward the hill that did not have a tow rope or a warming house or any of the fancy amenities that so many of the city parks had. But it did have a small concession stand he hoped to check out later. Had to try the hot cocoa, right?

"Beat you to the top."

What? He shook off his musing and chased after Dani. Wow, she was quick.

He slipped on a patch of ice and went nose first into the powder.

Dani glanced back, stopped, and hurried back to him. "You okay?" She extended an arm to help him up.

He grabbed her arm and pulled her down. "I am now." He leapt up, gripping tight to the sled, and aimed for the top of the hill.

"This means war," she called behind him.

"And I intend to win." He didn't slow, but still only beat her by a few steps.

She lined up her sled alongside his. "Race you to the bottom."

"You're on."

She leapt onto her toboggan and pushed off while he struggled to get his long legs situated. Clearly, this wasn't her first race.

Finally, he got himself folded onto the toboggan and pushed off. He leaned forward, trying to add speed, which he did, but Dani still pulled away and reached the bottom a good ten feet before he did. Both continued on several more feet before virgin powder slowed them and plowed over the top of their sleds.

"Beat ya!" Dani jumped up and danced around, her arms waving in the air in some hokey victory dance.

"I just spotted you one. Couldn't let you leave the day being skunked."

"Excuse me?" Her dance came to a halt and, hands on hips, she glared at him.

And his stomach went topsy turvy. *Really, Lang? A pretty girl looks at you and your insides get all mushy?* He stuffed that down and went nose to nose with her. "Four more races. Person who loses three out of five buys the cocoa."

She poked him in the chest. "You're on, buddy." And just like that, she took off for the hill.

Well, she wasn't going to beat him this time.

But she did.

And she pushed off before he even reached the top.

"Not fair!" He called after her as he jumped onto his sled, only to have it slip out from under him and race downward. Empty. While he landed hard on his backside.

At the bottom, his sled stopped a few feet short of Dani's. She looked at the empty sled, then up the hill, and burst out laughing. She raised a hand displaying two fingers then proceeded to climb toward him.

Leaving his sled behind.

He gestured to it then steepled his hands together and mouthed "Please?"

From here, he couldn't see her eyes clearly, but he was pretty sure she rolled them as she went back to retrieve his sled. She trudged up the hill, carrying both, and thrust his into his hands. "Sending it down by itself doesn't count."

"Oh, so that round didn't count? Sweet!"

"Uh-uh-uh. I'm up two to one and you're going to be buying the hot cocoa."

"Wrongo." He flexed his muscles, and she for sure rolled her eyes that time. "I'm about to make a comeback, so let's up the ante."

"Oh, really?" She set her sled on the ground and held it in place with a foot. "What do you have in mind?"

"Dinner tomorrow. After house hunting. Loser pays."

A grin slowly took over her face. "Are you asking me out, Austin Lang?"

Was that what he'd done? Oh, gosh, he had! "I, uh . . . " He scratched beneath his stocking cap. "I guess."

"Then challenge accepted." Grinning, she started getting onto her sled.

He grabbed her arm. "But first we need to set the ground rules."

"Rules?" She groaned.

"Yep." He set down his sled and, like Dani had, secured it with his foot. No way was he going to let it race down without him again. "Instead of a race, it's whoever goes the furthest at the bottom. And we start at the same time."

She tapped her chin as if considering, then offered her hand. "It's a deal. And know that I look forward to you treating me tomorrow."

"That's what you think." He gestured toward her toboggan. "After you."

She positioned herself. "Your gentlemanlike behavior will not fool me, Lang."

He laughed and sat as well. "Ready?"

"To beat your butt."

"Ha! On your mark, get set, go!"

She was off before he barely finished saying, "Set."

"Cheater!" He yelled as he took off. He could still beat her, though. Instead of leaning forward, he lay back hoping to be more aerodynamic. He raced down, flying over bumps, the cold air chapping his cheeks. And suddenly he was even with Dani. Then passing her just as the hill flattened out at the bottom.

And he kept zooming.

"Watch out!"

What? He inclined up and a tree raced toward him. Eyes wide, he tugged on the sides of the sled, leaned to the right, and then he tumbled in the snow, his sled flying over him.

Dani came to a stop several feet ahead of him as he stood.

And she burst out laughing. "You look like a walking snowman."

"I feel like one." He shook his arms and legs, trying to empty his sleeves and pants of snow that had somehow managed to climb inside everything he was wearing. Giving up, he threw his hands in the air. "Fine. You win. I buy dinner tomorrow."

"And I'll get the hot cocoa today." She walked back to him carrying her sled and dropped it by his feet. "Up for another run?"

"I'm up for dry clothes." He looked down and brushed off his jeans. When he looked up, her face was inches from his.

And suddenly he was sweating. Whew boy.

"You have some snow . . . " She took off a glove and wiped her hand across his cheek.

The way his body temperature skyrocketed, he could probably melt the entire hill. He cleared his throat, but his voice still came out octaves higher than it should. "Uh, should we get cocoa now?" He aimed for the tiny concession stand, trying to shake the image of Dani staring at him, her eyes hooded and her lips slightly separated.

"Hey." She hurried past him and pulled to a stop in front of him.

He braked just in time to prevent a collision.

Then she stepped closer.

Before he could back away, both of her hands were on his cheeks. "We make a good team, don't you think?"

Think? Not when the warmth of her hand reached from his ears to his toes and his brain had suddenly decided to take a vacation. "I, uh . . . " What? *Am extremely attracted to you?* Those words would not, could not, exit his mouth.

And then she stepped closer.

Heaven help him, his feet wouldn't move. She'd cast some kind of spell that had sunk his feet into concrete and amped up his heartbeat a hundred times quicker than normal.

Standing on tippy-toes, she raised her chin, angling toward

him, drawing him like a powerful magnet.

"Mommy, I beat Daddy!"

Something barreled into him, buckling his knees, and his mouth slammed into Dani's nose.

"Ow!"

He pushed away, and his eyes grew wide at the site of blood gushing from her nose, turning the snow at their feet into a horror scene. "I'm sorry, so sorry!" He reached into his pockets for a tissue.

"Help me find a seat." She pinched the bridge of her nose and leaned forward.

"Yeah, okay." He glanced around. There. A large firepit surrounded with benches. He grasped her hand. "This way."

She followed silently and without resistance then sat on a bench while leaning toward the fire.

"I'll get you a . . . a tissue." He hurried to the concession stand, and someone jogged toward him, a wad of tissues in her hand.

"I'm so sorry. Joel was just so excited he forgot to look where he was going."

"It's okay." Austin took the tissues and ran back to Dani. "Here you go." Little Joel's excitement probably saved him from making a bigger mistake than bashing into Dani's nose. "Are you okay?"

She nodded. "It happens all the time." Her voice was nasally. "You look at me funny, and I get a bloody nose."

"So that's what happened back there," he said, hoping she was as relieved as he about a kiss not happening. "I was looking at you funny."

"You're hysterical, Lang." She wiped her nose. "Talk about ruining a moment." She tossed the tissue toward a nearby trash can. "I can't seem to hit anything. The trash can. Your lips." Her head angled toward his.

He jerked his gaze away. He wouldn't exactly call their moment ruined, but the kid running into them at that exact time was providential. Not that he wouldn't have enjoyed kissing her, but the last thing he needed right now was a relationship, especially with his mother getting out of prison.

"I'm just glad you're okay. Oh, and the mom apologized for her son. Apparently, we weren't the only ones racing."

"Hmph. People should learn to control their kids." She wiped her nose again and laughed. "My mom would get a kick out of that statement."

He grinned. "You mean she couldn't control an angel like you?"

"Hard to believe, right?" She gave her nose another wipe and tossed the tissue toward the garbage can again. Missing again. "Well, I could use some of that hot cocoa about now."

"On my way."

Whew. He'd sidestepped that bullet, for now anyway. Maybe by the time they got back to his place she'd come to her senses and forget all about the near-kiss. Austin picked up Dani's tissues off the ground and threw them into the trash can. Or common sense would inform her that the last person a senator's daughter should date was a former homeless kid who'd been closer to being a convict than her tissues were to the garbage can.

## Chapter Eleven

*D*ani pulled onto the residential street leading toward Austin's home. In the driveway was his old Honda Civic, the vehicle he'd said had once been his home. Unfathomable. And to think she was worried about not getting a fancy enough, up-to-date enough vehicle. And home. No wonder he was fine in the studio he was renting and didn't give a hoot about popcorn ceilings. Knowing his story really put life into perspective.

And it attracted her to him even more.

She drove past several houses lit up with blinking lights.

After today, what was he thinking? Probably not about the near-kiss that seemed to mortify him, but rather about the home he had to buy and the woman he disdainfully called "Mom" who would be living there with him. For just a little bit today she'd gotten him to forget about all that. Tonight, they'd figure out what kind of home he needed, and she'd set up appointments for tomorrow and Monday. That would take a little bit off his mind.

But her thoughts kept darting back to flirting with him, and the adorable way he reacted. How refreshing it was to be with someone who didn't believe they were God's gift. Yeah, flirting might not have been the smartest thing she'd ever done. After all, he was her sort-of boss, plus he was hiring her to help find his house.

Still . . .

The guy had no clue how attractive he was. She'd never met anyone so real, someone who'd overcome so much. Growing up in the world of politics, people always wore a façade to win others over. Even her brother, the pastor, admitted struggling to be real as his congregants tended to put him up on a pedestal and didn't want to see the messed-up man he was. She could tell them a thing or two. Austin didn't need to wear masks, though there was plenty she didn't know about him. She couldn't wait to learn more.

She drove up the driveway and parked beside his Honda.

"I'll get your door." He had his door opened before she'd removed the keys from the ignition.

Oh, no he wouldn't. She got out before he had a chance to come around the car.

Shivering in the cooling October air, she retrieved her laptop from the trunk of her car.

"Ready?" He gestured toward his landlord's door.

Dani looked at the steps leading to Austin's apartment. "We're not going to your place?"

"One of Bea's rules is that I'm not allowed to have women over."

"Seriously? But I was at your place a few weeks ago."

"That was just for a moment."

"Wow." Dani shook her head. "That's . . . " She hesitated, not wanting to insult him. "That's really old-fashioned."

"I guess. But it's designed to keep me out of trouble." He grinned and gestured toward Bea's door again. "Not that I've had much opportunity."

Shaking her head, Dani walked side by side with Austin. "You mean to tell me you haven't had many girlfriends?" A good-looking guy like him would have women falling all over him.

He shrugged. "I haven't really dated. Haven't had time and I haven't met anyone that interested me."

Wow. She seemed to be saying or thinking that a lot around him. She couldn't count on her fingers and toes all the guys she'd gone out with, although she'd never dated anyone more than a couple of months. They'd all been as shallow as she.

They reached the door and Austin knocked. A few seconds later his landlord, a woman who looked to be in her sixties, answered the door. Her brows flitted up as her gaze flickered from Austin to Dani. "Austin. To what do I owe the pleasure?"

"Bea, this is Dani Chamberlain, my realtor. Mind if we borrow your kitchen table to do some house hunting?"

"Of course, you can." She gestured toward her living room. "So nice to meet you, Dani. Come on in."

Dani stepped inside the updated yet character-filled house that immediately felt and smelled like home, with some kind of baked treat filling the air with a tantalizing aroma. "Nice to meet you too, Bea." Dani offered her hand as the chocolatey scent made her mouth water. She removed her boots, set them on a mat, and hung her jacket on a coat tree, beside Austin's.

Bea gestured toward the kitchen. "Now you two make yourselves comfortable at the table. Once I get you settled, I'll stay out of your way."

"Appreciate it, Bea." Austin led Dani into a kitchen that whooshed Dani back in time. Tiny, all-white everything except the floors that were a black and white linoleum checkerboard. Formica countertops had a metal banding around the edges. The appliances were ancient yet still had that showroom shine.

Judging by the cookie-baking smell coming from the oven, the appliances worked well, too.

Dani set her bag on top of the Formica-topped table and pulled out her laptop. Time to get to work. She sat in a vinyl-covered chair and Austin sat beside her.

"Can I offer you two a hot beverage? Cocoa? Coffee? Apple cider?" Bea hovered over them.

"Apple cider sounds wonderful."

"Same here." Austin started to stand. "I can help—"

"You sit back down, young man. Let me have the honor of serving you."

Dani had heard her mother use the same phrase umpteen times, but never in a home context. And never directly to Dani. It was always to her constituents.

Yet, Dani knew her mom loved her. With the sound of the oven door opening and closing in the background, Dani opened her laptop and created a Word file to take notes. She tried logging on to the MLS site, but she wasn't hooked up to Wi-Fi here. Hopefully the older woman had internet. "Bea, can I get your Wi-Fi login and password?"

"Certainly, hon." Bea set mugs with steaming hot cedar in front of her and Austin. "The login is FBI Stakeout Van #121."

Dani couldn't resist laughing. "That has to be the most clever login I've heard of. I love it."

"You can blame Austin for that." Bea set a plate of six freshly-baked peanut-butter cookies on the table. "He thinks he's funny."

"Oh really?" Her mouth watering from the scent of the cookies, Dani sat back and eyed the stoic man seated beside her. "I didn't know you were a comedian."

"It's the quiet ones you have to watch out for." Bea patted Austin on the shoulder.

He just shook his head, but he was smiling.

"I'll leave you two alone. Austin will help you with the password. It's too complicated for me to remember."

"Thanks, Bea. We appreciate your help." *And your cookies.* Dani could no longer resist grabbing one and biting into it. She moaned with pleasure. Goodies like this were never baked in her home.

"Glad to do it for Austin here. The boy's like a grandson to me. Oh, and I've long admired your mother."

Dani choked on her cookie. So, the woman kept tabs on the Minnesota political scene. Dani shouldn't be surprised.

"Here you go, hon." Bea handed her a napkin.

Dani also wasn't surprised that Bea liked her mom who had every female vote in the state tied up. People loved her. Dani forced that smile that had been part of her public wardrobe growing up with a political mother. "I'll pass that on to her."

Bea left the kitchen.

Now they could get to work.

Oh, but first, the password. She clicked the internet access tab on her task bar then clicked FBI Stakeout Van #121. "Password?"

"Capital U." Austin's voice had a grin to it as he rattled off a series of letters, numbers, and characters that made no sense. "Get it?"

Dani hit enter. "Get what?"

"The password. You hack me, I call police." Austin laughed at his own joke.

"So that's what you do for fun? Make up stupid passwords?"

"Hey, I thought it was clever."

"Uh-huh. You just go on thinking that." Dani chuckled and brought up the Multiple Listing Service site. She put that on one side of her screen then her Word file on the other. "Okay, no more goofing around, let's find you a house. Is your budget the same as before?"

He sighed heavily. "Yep, but I would prefer less now that I'm going to be supporting my mom."

"Makes sense." Frustrated her too. "How many bedrooms?"

"Three now, for Mom, my sister, and me."

"Bathrooms?"

"Two. Can't imagine sharing a bathroom with my mom."

"I hear ya." Dani typed all that into her Word doc. "Location the same?"

"Preferably."

"So, there's a little wiggle-room?"

He shrugged. "Very little."

"Turnkey?"

"Nope. I'd even go for a fixer upper now if that'll get me into a bigger house. If I have questions, Richard's done a lot of construction, and his brother's a contractor, so I've got a few experts in my pocket."

She asked a few more questions, then began the search. Given his budget and parameters, it wasn't going to be easy, but she was always up for a challenge. By the end of the night, she had all day Sunday following church and Monday evening filled with showings for him. With only two months left until he had to move out, hopefully one of these would work for him.

"So that's it?" Austin snatched the final cookie from the plate.

Good thing, because she was about to take it, which would have made four cookies for her. That was three too many. But, oh, were they good!

She packed up her laptop while yawning. "Guess I better hurry home and get my beauty rest."

"So that's your secret?"

Her head jerked toward Austin, whose face was an adorable

shade of pink. "Did you just call me pretty?"

"I, uh . . . " He shrugged and flashed a lopsided smile. "Well you are."

"That's the nicest thing anyone's ever said to me."

"Come on, I know you've been told you're pretty before. You probably have guys falling at your feet."

"But none are as honest as you." She touched his cheek, darkened with a shadow of whiskers. "When you say it, I know you mean it here." She moved her hand from his cheek to his heart.

His Adam's apple did a slow bob and he scratched the back of his neck. Oh, he was adorable when flustered. But that was enough teasing for the moment, especially with Bea in the next room, so she pulled back her hand then pushed away from the table.

"I'll walk you to your car." He got up quickly, pushed both chairs in, and led her to the front door, past Bea watching the ten o'clock news.

Bea muted the TV. "Nice to meet you, Danielle. I hope to see you again."

"I'll be back." And maybe not just for house-hunting purposes, if she had her way.

The two put on their winter gear, then Austin waved to Bea before stepping outside with Dani.

The frigid air chilled her immediately. If Austin would put his arm around her, that would help immensely, but he walked toward her car with his hands tucked so far into his jeans it would take an excavator to dig them out.

She was up for the challenge.

She made a show of shivering as they walked the short sidewalk. "The temperature must have dropped twenty degrees."

"Winter's here, that's for sure." His hands didn't even flick in his pockets. Okay then, he wasn't taking the hint, so she'd try the direct approach. Some guys needed it spelled out for them.

She clicked her remote, starting the car, but she didn't unlock it.

Austin tried the door anyway, which she expected.

"You have a minute before I leave?" She leaned against her car and looked back at him.

"I thought you were cold."

"I wouldn't be if you put your arm around me." She couldn't be any more obvious than that.

"Dani . . . " His hands somehow plunged deeper into his pockets. They probably had holes from all the pocket digging he did. "I know what you're doing. It's not a good idea."

So, he wasn't clueless after all. "Why not? I like you, and you like me. We should see where that takes us."

"It's not that easy."

"Really? Why not? I know you wanted to kiss me earlier, and I definitely wanted to kiss you." She stepped closer to him and curved a gloved hand on his cheek. Thankfully, he didn't back away. "For the first time in my life, I've met someone real, someone good, and I really believe we make a good p—"

"Dani." He stepped closer to her, and she could feel his breath as he looked down at her. "We can't."

Her hand dropped to her side.

"You and I, it won't work, and you know it too. I'm just another project for you. My mom's getting out of prison and moving in with me. I don't even know who she is. And you don't really know who I am. Besides, if you really knew me, you'd know that I'm far from good. The smart thing to do is keep this . . . this relationship at a professional level."

He stepped away. "Goodnight, Dani. I'll see you here tomorrow."

He left her standing, shivering by her car, her mouth agape. She sniffled. He was not just another project, and by the end of their house hunt, he'd see what her heart really said.

## Chapter Twelve

*A*ustin remained at the bottom of the outdoor steps watching Dani's car back out of the driveway then screech as it zoomed down the road.

Then he stomped up the stairs, threw open the door to his apartment, removed his jacket and shoes, and clomped over to his daybed where he plopped down. Man, he hated hurting her, but she didn't realize he wasn't for her. Was he a cold-hearted idiot? No. He knew better than that. But he'd told her the truth, that they weren't a good match.

Besides, once she started thinking with her head instead of her heart, she'd see things his way.

He heard footsteps on the stairs outside his apartment and then a knock on his door. Who could that be? Not Dani. Even she wasn't that quick. He got up and hurried to open the door.

Bea? Wearing a big scowl and not carrying any cookies. Uh-oh. What had he done wrong now?

"Uh, come on in."

She swooped in, removed her gloves, and made herself comfortable in his recliner.

"Can I get you something to drink?" He walked to his kitchenette and pulled out a bottle of pop for himself. "I've got cookies. That you made."

"Child, you don't have to wait on me, just come sit down and have a chat."

Something told him he wasn't going to like this chat, but he obediently sat on the edge of his daybed, his hands braced on his knees. "Did I do something wrong? If you're worried about me getting mixed up with Dani, you shouldn't be. She's just my realtor. And if you're concerned about me finding a home in time, we've got a whole bunch of showings scheduled for the next couple of days."

"Are you done?" Bea folded her hands in her lap.

Austin shrugged.

"Just because I'm an old woman does not mean I still don't have my eyesight."

"Okay?"

"Young man, there was more electricity zapping between the two of you than what's heating this whole city."

Moaning, he pushed back on the daybed and slumped down. "There's nothing between us."

"I saw the two of you in my kitchen and by her car."

"You were spying on us?"

"As any self-respecting mom-figure should."

He laughed in spite of himself.

"Sure looked like something to me." She wagged a finger at him.

He groaned. "As I said, you don't have to worry about her. Yeah, I like her, and she said she likes me, but it can't happen."

"And why not?"

"Wait . . . You want us to get together?"

"A spitfire like her is exactly who you need."

He scratched his head. "Yeah, a spitfire I've known a grand total of one week."

"Ask her out, then. That's how you get to know someone."

"Well, for your information, I have asked her out. Tomorrow night, actually." Although, after his sorry demonstration a few minutes earlier, she'd probably tell him to take a hike. "But it's all business. You can't expect me and Dani to work out. In case you haven't heard, she's the daughter of a senator."

"So?"

"Hello. I'm the son of a convict who happens to be getting out in a few months. Do you think Dani will want to hang around me then?"

"Sounds like you're borrowing trouble."

"I used to be homeless."

"Used to be. And last I checked, Ms. Chamberlain is an advocate for the homeless."

"I should be in jail, and I would be if Richard and Sheila hadn't offered me mercy."

"And look at what grew from their mercy. A young man feeding and helping the homeless, a teacher giving the youth tools to be successful in life. To me, it sounds like Ms. Chamberlain chose a winner. You are both children of the King! Besides, the Word tells us in Galatians that 'There is neither Jew nor Greek, there is neither slave nor free, there is no male and female, for you are all one in Christ Jesus.' Are you going to argue with the Good Book?"

He slumped further. "No." But then, the Bible was exactly the tool supporting his argument. "The Good Book also tells us, in 2 Corinthians I believe, that we're not to be unequally yoked."

This time, Bea did the slumping. "She's not a believer? But her mother is, and her brother is a preacher."

"Honestly, I don't know where she stands with God, but I get the impression that the two of them aren't exactly close."

"That's the first good point you've made." Bea sat up and glanced toward the ceiling as if she was having a personal conversation with God right there. She even nodded in answer. Austin wouldn't be surprised if Bea's connection was that strong. He'd never met a godlier woman.

"So, we're good? No more lecture?"

"No lecture, but I do have homework for you, Mr. Teacher."

Despite himself, he grinned at her cleverness. "I happen to be a fan of homework."

"Good." Bea stood, and he got up as well. "You need to find out what Ms. Chamberlain believes, and if she's not a Christ follower, then certainly, keep your relationship platonic. But no one has a more powerful story to tell than you, young man. Who better than you to share the gospel with her?"

Austin flung his hands in the air. Arguing with Bea was useless, especially when everything she said was laced with wisdom. "Okay. I give."

"That's my boy, but also—"

"Another *but*? I thought we were done."

She wagged a finger at him. "When your students left the room at the end of the first trimester, were they done learning?"

"Of course not."

"Then think of this as the beginning of your next trimester with me."

He sighed. "I'm ready to learn."

"Good. Just know this. If Ms. Chamberlain is a believer, then your heart—" Bea tapped his chest with her finger "—and your head need to have a conversation about your feelings for her before someone gets hurt." She looked toward the window facing the street. "More than they already are."

Dani slammed her car door and stomped into her mom's house. She'd practically thrown herself at Austin. Twice! And he turned her down without breaking a sweat. No, that wasn't true. He was sweating all right, and that was what made her furious now. She needed to figure out a way to convince Austin that they were good together.

She threw her purse onto the kitchen island and searched the pantry for some comfort food. Her mom always kept chocolate around, though she tried to hide it, not wanting to admit she had a chocolate addiction.

*Ah, there's the stash.* Dani pulled an unopened, single-serving bag of peanut-butter M&M's from behind the flour container and hurried to the basement family room. She turned on the gas fireplace, brought up *While You Were Sleeping* on the big screen, and cuddled with a blanket on the chaise end of the sectional while eating her M&M's. Chocolate and a chick flick was the perfect recipe to forget her troubles, and maybe it would inspire her own romantic plans.

"I see I've passed along my bad habits."

Dani turned toward her mother coming down the stairs and displayed the bag of M&M's. "I'll share."

Her mother held up a new bag. "I think this is a full-bag movie."

"Is that good for your heart?"

"A treat now and then won't hurt me."

"As long as those treats are eaten in moderation."

"Sounds like you're trying to mother me."

Dani laughed at the role reversal. "Agreed."

Mom pulled up a foot stool, sat beside Dani, and shared the

blanket. "It's been a long time since we've done this. Remember when you were little, you, me, and Brad would sit down here all snuggled together?"

"I loved those times." And then her mom made it big in politics as an advocate for families. Then when her father died, her mom's popularity grew, especially among the single mothers struggling to feed and clothe their children.

And the quiet family moments disappeared along with her mom's blossoming career.

How ironic that to become a family advocate, she'd sacrificed her own family time.

Her mom pointed to the movie screen. "I just love how Lucy makes it on her own in spite of all her challenges."

Whoa. Where had that come from? Warning tingles shot from Dani's shoulders to her toes as she hit the pause button. "Are you trying to tell me something?"

"Not really. I'm just impressed with Lucy's fortitude."

"And not so impressed with mine."

"That's not what I said."

"It's what you implied." Dani pulled away from her mom and squeezed herself against the arm of the sectional, hugging her knees to her chest, wishing she could move further away.

"You're putting words in my mouth, as usual."

"So, you are proud of me?"

"Of course, I am, and I'll be even prouder when you move into your own place, using your own money."

Dani laughed at the realization. "So that's what this is about. I'll look for a place when you're doing better."

"You mean you haven't been looking? You only have a few weeks remaining to move."

"Seriously?" Panic sizzling through her pores, Dani threw off the blanket and leaped off the couch. "You just had a heart attack. You think I'm going to leave you here alone in this . . . " She spread out her arms. "This mausoleum?" That was exactly what the house would become if Dani left her mom alone.

"Danielle." Her mom remained on the couch, hands in her lap, as if this was an everyday conversation. "This is no surprise to you. I gave you a firm date to move out, and that hasn't changed."

"But . . . " She hadn't looked for a home, not since her mom's heart attack. Like always, she'd anticipated her family giving her the easy way out. Without looking at her mom, Dani paced the room, her heart sprinting faster than a mouse running from a cat. She felt like that mouse right now, running for her life, except her life could end up on the streets like those people in the tent city if she didn't do something.

"Darling, I just—"

Dani held up her hand, silencing her mom, and stopped pacing. Rejected by Austin and her mom in a matter of hours. She may as well shut down her heart completely and not care.

But she did care. Maybe too much. If only she could turn off her heart and passions and just follow the rules like normal people. If people and life didn't distract her from staying on task, she wouldn't get into these messes.

She looked over at her mother. Were her eyes glassy?

*Don't look. Don't let it matter to you.*

Rather, don't show that it really does matter.

She tilted up her chin and nodded toward the stairs. "I'm going to bed." She aimed for the steps.

"Danielle . . . "

Dani stopped and turned only her head but said nothing. Speaking would betray her emotions.

"Please know that this isn't easy for me. I do love you."

Kicking her daughter out of the home was one heck of a way to show love.

She turned from her mom and hurried up two flights of stairs to her temporary bedroom. Tomorrow, she'd focus on her job and not only find herself a place, but Austin too. One he could turn into a home for him and his mom so neither of them would be homeless again. All while not letting her attraction to him get in the way. It wouldn't be that much different than the silent treatment she excelled at.

Challenge accepted.

Seated on her bed, she texted Austin and told him she couldn't eat out tomorrow night. Something had come up. All she had to do now was avoid dining with him for the rest of the house hunt, until they each found a place to live.

No more distractions.

Which meant tonight she had to do her research and find a place for herself before she became homeless. In this tough rental market, that wasn't going to be easy, but she was up for that challenge too. But it wouldn't be nearly as tough as not flirting with Austin, because she was falling for him fast.

*Chapter Thirteen*

With Bea's words and Dani's flirting chasing around like squirrels in his brain, Austin found an old college notebook and ripped out a piece of paper. Time to say good riddance to those distracting squirrels and tell his mom exactly what he thought about her letter.

Visions of his so-called mom chasing away Bea and Dani dashed through his brain, so he put pen to paper, spewing angry words then crossing them out:

*December 2*

*Hey Mom,*

*This is Austin. ~~Well, I guess you know that already from the return address.~~*

*~~Wanted to let you know~~ I got your letter, ~~and honestly, it ticked me off. I don't know how you think, after what you put Brittany and me through, that you can just tell me you're moving in with me and expect everything to be okay, because it's not.~~*

*I've worked ~~my tail off~~ hard these past years, ~~digging out from being homeless. No thanks to you,~~ I got my GED then graduated from college with a teaching degree. ~~Yeah, you read that right. I'm a~~ ~~teacher. And a good one too. And I had my whole life~~ ~~together, was planning to buy a home, e~~ Even met a woman I like ~~and then like some horror movie, you~~ ~~show up.~~*

*~~Yeah. I lived in that broken-down car you gave me~~ ~~until I met people with real character. People who~~ ~~know what it means to parent. Unlike you.~~*

*Brittany's now down in Florida with her foster parents, going to college. ~~Rather ironic, cuz when I~~ ~~came to visit you five years ago, I stole from the~~ ~~people who loved me (thanks to your 'education') and~~ ~~planned to run away with Brit to Florida and start a~~ ~~new life. But I couldn't.~~*

*~~Because God tells us to honor our parents, I guess~~ ~~I have to let you~~ You can come live with me. ~~I'm not~~ ~~happy about it, but it is what is it. Just so you know,~~ ~~you won't be getting a free ride from me.~~ But know, there will be rules.*

*~~Guess I'll s~~ See you in March.*
*Austin.*

He rewrote the letter, leaving out the crossed-out words, and debated taking out the bit about Dani, but left it in to show he'd moved on. Feeling much better than he had this morning, he tucked his letter into an envelope, stamped it, and put it in the mail. Maybe by the time she got out, she'd change her mind about moving in with him.

*December 10*

*Hi Mom,*

    *Austin again.*

    *Since we'll be living together soon, I figured it's not a bad idea for us to get to know each other better, make the transition easier.*

    *I do want to be a good son to you, but I admit, it's not going to be easy. I'm dealing with a lot of anger toward you that I'm working on forgiving. I'm grateful God gave us a few months to prepare.*

    *Well, I guess that's all I have to say now.*

    *Will write again soon,*

    *Austin*

## Chapter Fourteen

*D*ani steeled herself before walking through the dining hall door for the Family Table Meal. These past couple of weeks had been tough working alongside Austin, both here and looking for a home. If only he knew how hard it was for her to rein in her emotions. But until this house hunt was done, she had to focus on business. The minute she started flirting with him, he'd get all flustered and his face would turn the cutest shade of red which told her he cared for her too. And then she'd get her hopes up too high about a possible future with him.

As long as she lived with her mother, she couldn't chance a broken heart. Those types of emotions needed to be shared with a jacuzzi and a tub of cookie dough in a place she could call her own.

She stepped into the room and her gaze flew to the kitchen. Austin was there, of course, manning the stove. Apparently, chili was on the menu today. Chili and toasted cheese sandwiches. That would warm the diners for a little bit anyway.

Austin turned around and his gaze slid right past her.

Pinching her heart. It shouldn't. That was what she wanted, right?

But then his gaze flicked right back to her, and he smiled.

Setting loose the butterflies in her stomach. Oh, dear. She returned a businesslike smile, but that took every mouth-muscle she had. She looked away first and walked toward the kitchen where most volunteers had already gathered. Joe, Austin's Santa-like assistant, divvied up the day's assignments—Dani volunteered for serving again so she could reconnect with a few people, especially Sammi—then Austin led the group in prayer.

Without saying a word to Austin, she set about serving the diners. She actually loved talking with the people and listening to their stories. Some talked about their families they hadn't seen for years. One person bragged about the executive position he once held in a Fortune 500 company. Sammi told her to "Get lost."

Too many diners lamented that they'd be spending Christmas alone, and that broke her heart.

Yes, her relationship with her mother was complicated, but they did love each other. While Dani complained about being "kicked out" and being "homeless" soon, the truth was she had plenty of viable options. She was just picky. Which meant she needed to modify her own home search to fit her current budget, not the mommy's-supporting-me budget.

Dani hated admitting it, but her mom had done the right thing in booting her out. She wasn't going to be homeless and hungry, not like the people in this room.

A meal was going to be served here on Christmas Day, and practical gifts such as wool mittens, socks, and scarves would be given out. Austin had told her he wasn't planning on working here on Christmas day, but that didn't mean Dani couldn't. She'd ask her mom and aunt and uncle to join her. Now that would be a Christmas to remember.

Would Sammi be there? One way to find out.

She brought Sammi a small plate with a couple of chocolate-covered donuts and sat down across from her. "How was the chili?"

"Hot."

In spite of herself, Dani laughed. A smile even snuck a peek from Sammi's lips. The first sign of victory Dani had seen with Sammi.

Which meant talking to these people did make a difference. "Will you be here on Christmas Day?"

"Don't know."

"Well, I hope to see you." Dani jotted a mental note to purchase several fast-food gift cards to give out. She could probably talk her mom and aunt and uncle into contributing as well.

Sammi took a large bite of a donut and spoke with her mouth full. "I'll be here."

Dani startled and had to hold in her excitement. Taking a chance, she reached across the table and touched Sammi's hand. "I look forward to seeing you." Then she got up and rushed to the kitchen. She couldn't wait to tell Austin about her breakthrough!

"Hey, Austin, you'll never guess—"

He held up a hand, silencing her, as he showed a new volunteer where to put the clean dishes.

This news was worth waiting to tell.

Finally, Austin was finished with the volunteer and looked at her. "Can I help you?"

That was it? No 'Hi, how's it going?' No 'Good to see you.' No cute or awkward smile. Just a businesslike "Can I help you?"

And that stung. Had she taken her business-only attitude too far? Maybe, but she had to keep their relationship at a professional level if she wanted to find homes for each of them.

Otherwise, Austin was far too distracting.

She dug her community service form from her pocket and handed it to him, wearing as straight a face as she could muster. "I'd like this signed please."

"Sure thing." He took the form then looked around. "Got a pen?"

"No. I was told not to bring my purse."

"Oh. Yeah." He found a pen in one of the drawers and signed her form. "I'll see you on Monday to look at more homes?" Then he smiled.

Butterflies tangoed in her stomach, but she did not return the smile. "I'll pick you up, six o'clock sharp." They better find their homes soon, or she'd probably chase him away for good.

*December 16*

*Hi Mom,*

*Have you gotten my letters? I've written a couple so far. I'd like to hear back from you.*

*Merry Christmas a week early. You should be receiving your gift soon. Hope you like books. Do you have any kind of celebration? I usually spend it with my mentor and his family in New York, but I'm too busy to make the trip this year. (And no, I don't make the kind of money to fly a lot—the plane tickets were always a Christmas gift.) My landlady's going out of town, too, so it'll be a quiet Christmas for me. And that is okay.*

*Just so you know, for the past month I've been looking for a house. My budget isn't very big, and Christmas is coming up soon, so people aren't selling homes. I'll find something though. My realtor is doing the best job she can considering the current market.*

*Um, speaking of my realtor, in my first letter I mentioned liking someone. Well, she's my realtor. And she volunteers with me at Family Table—we serve meals to the homeless. I thought she liked me— she flirted a lot the first couple of weeks—but now,* she's all business. Guess it's my fault for not flirting back. But I don't know how.

Problem is, I like her. And the more time I spend with her, the more I like her, but I get brain freeze when she talks to me, and now I don't know if she even likes me.

I know. Stupid, right?

Anyway, my landlady told me I better make a move soon or Dani'll find someone else. Maybe I'll ask her to Christmas Eve service at church. Would that be lame? I have no clue.

Yeah, I know. TMI from your son, right? It just feels good to 'talk' to someone about Dani.

Anyway,

Merry Christmas!

I'll write again soon.

Austin

## Chapter Fifteen

*A*ustin wasn't usually one for wasting time at the mirror, but today was different.

These last couple of weeks had flown past too quickly. Three-plus weeks of house hunting and Family Table Meals and spending time with Dani, and she'd turned off her flirt as quickly as she'd turned it on. He needed to apologize tonight, and hopefully the Dani he first met would reappear.

Oh, Dani had been nice and helpful, but not flirty. Right or wrong, he missed it. He was crushing and hurting bad.

Should he slap on some aftershave? Maybe add a little gel to his hair? Nah, that would be too obvious, and not him. Dani liked him for being real, and that was who he'd be today, even with his heart pumping faster than he'd fallen for Dani.

The button-up shirt, new jeans, and clean-shaven look would have to do. He had to make a move. Now. If he didn't have the guts to invite Dani to Christmas Eve service coming up on Sunday, he'd be attending alone. Richard was home in New York. Brittany was staying in Florida. Bea was going out of town for the weekend. Normally, Austin wouldn't mind going alone, but now that he'd met Dani?

Hopefully, she'd finally forgive him for rejecting her two weeks ago.

He inhaled slowly and released it to the count of ten, hoping to calm his racing heart. Today was about finding a house, not about finding someone to share it with.

Or was it?

He shook that thought away as he heard a knock on the door. His gaze flew to the clock. Twelve forty-five? That made her fifteen minutes early. Huh.

He hurried to the door and opened it, and a brisk wind blew in. The woman shivering there in the frosty air wasn't the carefree woman he was used to seeing. No, Dani looked all business today—from black flats to black padfolio to uncolored, unsmiling lips—which, considering showing him homes was her job, that was okay, but still, he wanted back the woman she'd been before he rejected her.

"Come on in. I just need to grab my wallet."

"I'll wait here, thank you." Even her tone was all business.

Which meant she still hadn't forgiven him. Oh boy. Why did he have to be such an idiot when it came to romance?

He'd apologize in the car, and by the end of the day maybe she'd forgive him. Oh, and it would be nice if they found a house too. Duh!

He grabbed a jacket from his closet and his wallet from his bedside table. "I'm ready."

"Good. We've got a lot of homes on our schedule today, so I figured getting an early start would be prudent."

Prudent? That wasn't a Dani word at all. Time to make amends.

"Actually, since you're early, do you have a minute to talk?"

Something flashed in her eyes, just a hint of the mischievous woman he had a crush on. She checked her Smart Watch and, without smiling, she shut the door behind herself and said, "One minute."

Whew. Okay.

He tucked his hands into his pockets and walked toward her, stopping about a yard away. "About what I said a few weeks ago . . . "

"That's behind us." She clutched the padfolio over her chest like a shield over her heart. "I was a fool and unprofessional, and you let me know."

"No, Dani." He stepped closer. "I was the idiot." He shook his head. "I've never had a girlfriend. Don't know the first thing about women, so I'm walking in completely unfamiliar territory. I realize, thanks to Bea, that I hurt you, but I didn't intend to." He took another step closer. "The fact is, I do care for you. I'm still sorting out what that means, but I'd really like to give us a chance."

Her expression remained neutral, and she kept the folio tight against her. "Let's see how today goes, shall we?" She motioned toward the door.

And Austin sighed. "Okay. Let's go find me a house." And by the end of the day, he hoped to uncover Dani's heart again too.

Dani hurried down the steps and to her car. Restraining her flirt had taken every muscle in her body. Austin had stood there looking so innocent and real, it had broken the flimsy chains off her heart. Oh, she was a goner. But she also had a job to do, a job that would help pay for her own rent, and she couldn't do it well if she let Austin distract her more than he already was. But as soon as she found each of them a home—hopefully tonight—then she'd let Austin know how she really felt.

Austin got in Dani's car, and it took every muscle in his body not to slam the door. She probably thought he was the biggest idiot in the world. That was what he got for letting stupid feelings take over. That would not happen again.

He'd apologized. Acceptance was up to her. Finding the right house was up to both of them. And then there was that important assignment Bea had given him to find out where Dani stood with Jesus.

It was going to be a busy and important day.

Dani got in the car and handed over a folder containing flyers of the homes she'd scheduled showings for. The plan was to get to them all, but sometimes reality got in the way.

Fifteen silent minutes later they parked in front of a Tudor that leaned more than the Tower of Pisa.

"Nope." Didn't even need to go inside. He wanted a fixer-upper, not a tearer-downer.

The second house had three bedrooms. Sort of. The third one wasn't any bigger than a walk-in closet and would barely fit a twin bed. The third house fit all his criteria but was too inner city. Too close to the life his mom needed to stay away from. He didn't want anything that would tempt his mom back to her addiction.

"Am I being too picky?" Austin tucked away the flyer for the inner-city home as Dani pulled away from the curb. "I mean, if it were just me and my sister, I'd have loved that one."

"Far from it." She glanced at the GPS map on her phone. "The problem is, when we list houses, we only put their sterling qualities, so we end up looking at a lot more than necessary."

"Sort of like dating."

Finally got a smile out of her. "Yeah, a lot like dating." She sat up straight and lowered her voice. "What's next on our Match-House.com list?"

He studied the top flyer and couldn't stop a smile. "It's new on the market. Does that mean it's just come off a broken relationship?"

Dani laughed. Oh, he'd missed that sound. "Might have to be leery of that."

"Right? Um, she's move-in ready, so the new owner can take quick possession. Oh, and she's a looker. She's got great curb appeal and is all updated with shiny stainless-steel appliances and granite countertops. Let's see . . . she's low maintenance, apparently. The HOA fee takes care of yard work and snow shoveling."

Austin tapped his finger on the sheet. "I know I said I'd like a home with an HOA when we first started, but now avoiding it is a way to save money."

"I'll keep that in mind for future showings. What else can you tell me about our match?"

"Says it's cozy. Keyword for small. It's only a thousand square feet."

"Too tight for you?"

"With Mom living there?"

"Yeah, that would be tight."

So why were they going to see it? Well, Dani knew her stuff. He'd have to trust her judgment. "She likes to have fun, too. Says the backyard is an entertainer's paradise."

Again, Dani laughed.

He'd do whatever he could to keep that going. "Now, this is different. Says owner would consider a rent-to-own situation. Don't know if that sounds like a promising relationship, if you ask me."

"Oh, you're right. All it would take would be one broken water heater and bye-bye renter." She flung a hand in the air. "Definitely not good for a long-term relationship."

"We still going to look at it? Sounds more like your kind of home than mine. It only has two bedrooms, one and a half baths, with no basement or attic to expand in."

"Let's look anyway." She tapped her fingers on the steering wheel. "You never know."

He shrugged. "You're the driver." But to him, it was a waste of time.

Twenty minutes later they parked in front of a well-kept townhome. They walked down a short sidewalk that cut between neatly-blown mounds of snow. Dani freed the key from the lockbox and opened the door. This home was a looker inside too. Open concept. Newly polished hardwoods. Fresh paint on the walls. Stainless steel appliances. No popcorn ceilings. But like the flyer said, it was . . . cozy.

"What do you think?" Dani removed her shoes and set them by the door.

Austin shrugged. "Small. Could use some paint."

"What?" She turned to him, her brows furrowed. "Why? It's freshly painted."

"Yeah, in grey and white. Feels like I'm stepping into a hospital or a black and white photo." Even the artwork was black and white and boring. Bleh.

"Shows what you know." She stuck her nose in the air, flung a hand through her hair, and talked in a snooty voice. "This is the modern look all millennials are craving."

"They want to live in a black and white life?"

"No, no, no." She wagged her finger. "That's just so the background doesn't interfere with a colorful life." She gestured toward the stairs. "Let's take a look."

Austin remained by the door, his winter shoes still on his feet. "You know, Dani, I feel like I'm wasting both your and the homeowner's time."

She splayed her hands. "Humor me."

"If you say so."

Dani led him upstairs where they checked out a master bedroom with a closet that would fit his daybed and his dresser, along with all his clothes. The bathroom had a soaker tub and a shower with a bench. The second bedroom and bath were small and painted in the same boring lack of color.

In spite of what Dani said, if he moved in here, every wall would get a makeover.

They returned to the main floor.

Dani turned in a slow circle, her gaze seeming to take in everything. "Well?" She slipped a foot into one of her shoes. "What do you think?"

He shrugged. "Before I knew about Mom, this would have made my 'maybe' list, but now it's just too small. There'd be no place for me to get away from her. No place for Brittany to stay, unless I gave her the master bedroom closet."

"Oh, she'd love that."

He snorted. "Her fosters have spoiled her beyond anything I can give her."

"Okay then. But I had to show you anyway. You just never know." She pulled her phone from her handbag then handed her car keys to Austin. "Would you mind warming the car? I need to check on something."

"Sure." Austin took the keys, went to the car, and turned it on. Well, that was a different showing. Usually the homes she took him to had some promise, but this one didn't fit him at all.

Twenty minutes later she finally joined him. Her step seemed much lighter coming out than it been had going in. She almost looked like the Dani he'd first met.

As usual, that turned his brain into mush, and he could think of nothing to say.

She got into the car. "Sorry I took so long, but I know another client who'd love that place, so I had to take care of some business." She attached her phone to its cradle and punched in the next address then turned to him and smiled the smile that caused chaos in his stomach. "Now my focus is completely on you. Fifteen minutes and we're at the next home."

She hummed all the way to the next stop, then it took all of thirty seconds for them to enter that place and leave. Some animal had turned the house into its own nest, and it reeked. It would take months, years to air it out.

Which left two more homes to look at today. Hopefully one would be right. He was tired of looking. Tired of sitting beside Dani and have her treat him like just another client, even though her attitude had improved since the monochrome house. Making a potential sale probably helped.

Still humming, Dani pulled to the curb of the next house, a story-and-a-half, brick-fronted home. Separate two-car garage. That would be a bonus. The large front yard could use some TLC, but nothing he couldn't handle. So far, this one showed promise.

Except for one important fact. He tapped the home's flyer. "It only has two bedrooms. Didn't we just talk about this?"

"Trust me." She waved her hand and began to open her car door.

He didn't move. "That's what you said a couple houses ago."

"I know, I know. Big mistake." She opened her door more. "Trust me on this one. There's a reason I chose it."

"You said that last time, too." He tried to cover the complaint with a smile, not wanting Dani to think him a whiner. So instead, like a good boy, he walked to the house alongside her.

They entered through the front door, stepping into a snug foyer big enough for one. To their left was a living room with hardwood floors that could use refinishing, but otherwise looked in decent shape. A floor-to-ceiling brick fireplace anchoring the living room wall looked to be in perfect condition. He'd love a fireplace to sit in front of and read. Built-in shelves flanking the fireplace would be a perfect spot to store all his books. The room wasn't overly large but would easily fit his daybed, recliner, and TV.

A cozy dining room, that was plenty big enough for a six-seater table, was adjacent to the living room.

"Thoughts?"

"So far, so good." He peeked into the entry closet that might squeeze in a half dozen winter coats. Plenty big.

She led him to an eat-in kitchen. It didn't have much countertop space, but it did have a lot of cabinets. Maybe if he got a mobile island, that would work for cooking and baking.

The appliances were white, but clean, and the floor was linoleum. The entire first floor needed a paint job, but the important thing was, the structure looked sound. She showed him the two bedrooms and one bath on the main floor. They weren't large, and the closets weren't any bigger than the one in the home's entrance. Neither he nor his mom would have need for bigger closets.

He opened cabinets, checked out the appliances, turned on faucets and the shower, flushed the toilet. Everything seemed to be in working order. "This is doable."

Dani elbowed him. "Or in Austin-speak, does that mean

fabulous?"

"No. It still only has two bedrooms."

"Well, here's where you use your imagination." She pointed to a door in the dining room.

"Okay." He opened the door to find steep stairs leading upward to a raftered attic. Interesting. He took the lead and climbed the steps and stopped when he reached the top. The space was plenty big enough for a large bedroom and second bath. The angled roof line would give the room character, and he would have plenty of storage in the slanted walls.

"What do you think?" Dani stopped beside him, close enough for him to smell her perfume, some subtle but fruity fragrance, and he itched to take her hand. Not yet, though. Not until he regained the ability to speak intelligently around her.

"This has potential. Let's check out the basement." His voice crackled as he hurried to the main floor, through the dining room, kitchen, and down the steps to the basement, where he stopped.

Now this wasn't bad either. The open concrete space housed an aging furnace, the water heater and softener, and the washer and dryer. And a whole bunch of spiderwebs. But it would make a perfect man cave. "How much is this house?"

She told him, and he cringed. It was a tiny bit over his max budget.

"But it's been on the market a while. I think I can talk them down."

"Then let's do it." Now, before someone snatched it away from him.

"Right now? We haven't seen the last house."

"Don't need to. I've seen enough to know this is the one I want."

"Then let's make an offer."

They sat at the dinette table and filled out paperwork with his offer. Dani's eyes twinkled like the Christmas lights blinking outside as she hummed Christmas music.

She signed her name with a flourish and threw down the pen and called the seller's agent with his offer. "Now we wait."

"How about we wait at dinner. I still owe you for losing the sledding race."

"That's right, you do! I know a little Chinese place nearby that's amazing."

"You're the driver."

She practically danced to her car. Selling houses obviously made her happy. If only he could light that same smile on her face.

A few minutes later they were seated in a private booth at a restaurant decorated with twinkle lights and garland. Christmas music played in the background enhancing the seasonal mood. Dani's phone sat in the middle of the table as they waited for a return call from the seller's agent. Not that they'd respond today. Or even tomorrow.

He and Dani placed their order, and then it was time for the talk Bea had encouraged him to have long ago.

"Can I ask you a question?"

"I need to talk—" Dani said at the same time. "You go first."

"Um." He fiddled with a napkin and was suddenly perspiring in spite of the cold weather. He was such a dork when it came to this dating thing. "I don't know exactly how to ask this without sounding arrogant or weird, but I'm wondering what your relationship with God is."

She shook her head, as if she hadn't heard correctly or she expected something else. "My relationship with God?"

"Um, yeah." His jittery hands moved from the napkin to his lap. "I know your mom's a believer, and your brother's a pastor, yet with all the time we've spent together this past month, I have no clue where you stand."

Her lips pursed. "I believe, if that's what you want to know. I believe that Jesus died and rose again. I believe I'm a messed-up person who needs His salvation." She shook her head and clenched her fists on the table. "But I'm also . . . mad. He took my dad when I was really young, and my mom's been so busy placating her constituents that she barely knows I'm around. Oh, and she's kicking me out of the house."

"Still? Even after her heart attack? Is she okay to live by herself?"

| "That's what I asked, and she said she was fine. It's all some big lesson"—she made air quotes—"she's trying to teach me."

"So, you're angrier with your mom than with God."

She sat back against the padded booth, saying nothing.

Maybe if he gave her more about himself, she'd open up. "Let me tell you my story. When Brit and I were young, we lived with Grandma. Mom would show up here and there, always choosing drugs over us. Then Grandma died." He looked away to hide the tears that always sprouted when he thought of his grandma. If not for her, no doubt he'd be in jail today. "We followed Mom as she flitted from boyfriend to boyfriend, and the last boyfriend made her choose between him and us. I don't have to tell you who she chose."

Dani's eyes squeezed closed. "I am so sorry. I can't imagine."

"I'm glad you can't. But we were lucky. Grandma taught Brit and me about God. I didn't see Him, though, until I aged out of the foster system and was living in my car. It was then God showed up big time."

"While you were homeless?"

"Yep." He nodded. "It was about this same time of year, I mugged a woman to get her purse."

Dani's eyes widened, and she seemed to sink into the booth's cushioned back. Hopefully she wouldn't be afraid of him now.

"It was Sheila. Richard's wife."

"Wait . . . " She shook her head. "Your family? They took you in after you mugged her? Unbelievable."

"Right? But I wasn't satisfied with that. Nope. I stole from them and planned to run away with my sister."

"But you couldn't."

"I wasn't a believer yet, but when God gets ahold of you . . . " He wouldn't let Austin run away. Rather, God ran to him.

"Guess I'm waiting for that to happen." She looked down at the empty table.

"I think He already has, Dani." He spread his open hands on the table. "I see it when you work at Family Table, when you were at the tent city, even out showing homes. He's got you, Dani, just like He had me."

"It's hard to imagine Him running to me, especially when I've blamed Him for everything that's gone wrong in my life."

"It is hard. I agree. But He doesn't treat us how we deserve, and that's mercy. When Richard and Sheila took me in after what I did to them, they showed me what mercy looks like. Now I get to extend that same mercy to my mom when she comes home, which is why getting the right place is so important to me."

Dani's eyes looked glossy as she reached across the table and took Austin's hands. "You're a good man, Austin Lang."

His cheeks burned, and he looked down. "Any chance you'd—"

The phone buzzed in the middle of the table.

His gaze flicked to Dani, and he nodded.

She picked up the phone and swiped right. "This is Danielle." She smiled while listening.

Good news?

"That's wonderful."

Definitely good news! The house was his!

More business talk and then finally she said "goodbye" and did a tiny dance in her seat.

"I got the house?" He felt like doing a dance too.

She winced.

And he slumped. So, he didn't get it?

"Actually, that was about the house I'm going to buy. Or rent to buy. I move in the end of the month."

He sat speechless, then it all made sense. "The black and white house. That was for you."

She grimaced as the server brought their food. "I should have told you, but I rather enjoyed watching you wonder if I knew what I was doing by showing you a place that obviously wouldn't fit you."

"Well, I'm happy for you." And disappointed for himself. Pure selfishness. "I can't wait to see how you brighten up the place." Hoping to hide his disappointment, he brought a spoonful of chow mein to his mouth and moaned. "This is good."

"Told you so." She took a bite of her moo goo gai pan. "And now we wait—"

The phone buzzed again, and Dani glanced at the caller I.D. "This is it."

"My place this time?"

She nodded. "Let's see if you got yourself a house."

# Chapter Sixteen

*A*ustin was always hungry. Except for right now as he watched Dani's face for clues while she chatted with the seller's realtor and took notes on a napkin. Her brows had crept close together, and her mouth was pinched. His offer wasn't that bad, was it? Especially when the house had been sitting vacant for weeks.

He tried a bite of his chow mein, but it stuck in his throat. He hated this house-buying process. Hated that even while in prison his mom dictated what he could buy. Honoring your parents shouldn't be this difficult.

Finally, Dani hung up.

"Well?" He dropped his fork, splattering his meal on the table. At the moment, he didn't care.

She shook her head and rolled her eyes. "They didn't accept your offer."

"I knew it." He shoved his plate to the center of the table. "So now what, do we keep looking?"

She laughed.

Laughed! When his future home was on the line. Dani had never been homeless.

He never wanted to be again.

"And here I always thought I was the drama queen." Dani

spooned a generous helping of her moo goo gai pan and ate it.

Man, she knew how to tie him in knots.

He rolled his shoulders, loosening tension-knotted muscles. "Okay, fine. I'm calm now. What do we do next?"

"They countered your offer."

"And you couldn't have told me that right away?"

"I was having too much fun watching you cringe." She ate another spoonful of her meal and sighed her pleasure.

He wished he had an appetite. "And . . . ?"

She finally put her spoon down and awoke her phone. "Your offer plus five-thousand dollars."

"Five-thousand?" Slumping, he shook his head. "That takes me out of my comfort zone. It may not seem like a lot to you, but to me, that's a new car. Money for repairs."

She held up her hand. "Hey, this isn't the end. You can counter."

"Oh." He blinked. "That's right." He curved both hands around the back of his neck and kneaded the knots. How could she sit there so calmly? "What do you suggest?"

"What are you comfortable with?"

"My original offer."

She shrugged and raised her hands.

"Okay. How about my original offer plus two-thousand, but that's it? That's my max. If they want more, the deal's done."

"That's fair." Dani called the realtor again and relayed Austin's counter. Now the waiting game began again.

He stared at barely-touched food. It didn't look appealing and the smell curdled his stomach. He couldn't remember the last time he hadn't been hungry, while Dani had finished half her plate.

She scooped another spoonful and held it midair while

watching him, then she lowered her spoon. "Why don't we get to-go boxes and occupy ourselves with something else?"

"It's a plan."

A few minutes later, their food was boxed up and paid for and they ventured out into the flurry-filled night.

After putting their food in Dani's car, they walked side by side on the sidewalk of the mini-mall strung with Christmas lights. Dani pointed to a children's playground across the road. "How about that?"

"Oh, real mature."

"And exactly what you need to do when you're doing stressful adult stuff like buying a house." She grabbed his arm and practically dragged him across the slush-covered street brightened by Narnia-like street lights. Beneath the lights, snowflakes danced to a tune only God could hear. They hurried to the park framed with snow-flocked pine trees.

True to Dani's word, his tension eased away. He grasped Dani's gloved hand and aimed for the circular slide. "This way."

She laughed and gripped his hand tighter.

They reached the slide and he gestured to the chain-like ladder leading upward. "After you." While she climbed, he began brushing off the slide. Just as he wiped the last of the snow, Dani hurtled toward him, knocking him backward, and landing on top of him.

"Ouch!" He feigned pain.

Her already large eyes grew rounder. "Are you okay?"

He pushed her off into the snow. "I am now." He ran for the ladder and a snowball pelted the back of his neck, sending melting flakes down his jacket. He jerked around and knelt, keeping his eye on her as she backed away, grinning. "You're in for it now." He patted together a snowball and hurled it toward her, splatting just below her chin.

"Well, you're not very gentleman-like." She brushed off the snow while bending to form another snowball.

And another.

And more until they both lay on the ground, covered with snow from hat to boot.

Laughing.

Austin couldn't remember a time he'd laughed like this. Life was too serious, and he'd worked too hard to get where he was.

But . . .

Didn't God invent fun?

He stood and offered his hand to Dani.

Who tried tugging him to the ground, but he planted his feet and pulled her up.

Close enough to melt all the snow from their jackets.

His heart suddenly beating faster than the snowflakes falling, his downward gaze caught her honey brown eyes and his breath stopped. He took off his glove and touched her cold-reddened cheek. "Thank you for breathing life into me."

Those captivating eyes smiled, and her lips parted ever so slightly as she inclined toward him.

He bent toward her.

And her phone rang out the "Happy" song.

"Seriously?" Dani flung her head back and tugged the phone from her pocket.

Austin just stood there, mouth agape as she chatted on with the caller, and the snow floated down thicker, faster. Whoever was on the phone had better have a good reason for messing up his moment, like his offer and been accepted, or her brother was coming home, or her mom had changed her mind about Dani's moving, or—

"You got the house!"

"What?" He shook his head.

She hit a few tabs on her phone and pocketed it. "There. Now we won't be disturbed." She stepped close to him again.

But he backed away. "I got the house?"

"Mm-hmm." She gripped his jacket, pulled him close, and looked up at him.

He was going to be a homeowner!

He wrapped both arms around the woman who'd made it happen and thanked her without words as he brushed his lips over hers then whispered in her ear. "You're amazing." His lips feathered across her suddenly warm check and back to lips eager to claim his. With a moan he took the kiss deeper, and she answered, making his body heat from his lips to his toes.

So, this was what it felt like to open his heart, not only to love, but to be loved.

If he could help it, he'd never close off his heart again. Maybe he was worthy of being loved.

Oh. My. Goodness!

Austin's kiss melted the freeze from her toes and fingers. And he was inexperienced? Whew. The man could take her to school.

Well, he was a teacher.

An hour—or a minute—later, definitely too soon, he pulled away and rested his forehead against hers. His lips bent into a smirk and he whispered, "How was that for a thank you?"

"I don't think it was quite enough." She entwined her hands behind his neck and tried pulling him toward her again.

But he ducked from beneath her hands then gripped them

with his. "We're wet and sweaty and it's cold out here, and you should go home and change before you catch a cold."

"I never get sick."

"That's good, because I'd like you to come to the Christmas Eve service with me."

"And here I thought you were going to ask me on a date."

"Sounds like a perfect first date."

"So, are you asking me out?"

He shrugged. "Could be."

"Hmmm. Let me think." She pulled out her phone and brought up the calendar while envisioning a kiss beneath the mistletoe. Her activist friends planned to protest something Christmasy in the Twin Cities. Probably a manger scene on a public property.

She didn't agree with the cause but knew it would upset her mom, so she'd planned to join them. Her mom wouldn't be the only one upset—imagine what Austin would think of her if she protested a nativity. Oh, she was a selfish brat.

Then here was Austin, whose mom had abandoned him and was in prison, yet he was writing her letters and opening up his home because it was the right thing to do. She'd never met someone so selfless.

Why would he even look twice at someone like her? Everything she did was about padding her ego.

Until she met Austin and Bea and even Sammi.

And to think, Austin liked her.

"Knock knock."

Dani shook her head as Austin broke into her daydream. "Sorry about that. I was just thinking about you and me."

"Pleasant thoughts I hope?"

"If toe-curling kisses are pleasant."

"Toe curling? Is that good?"

"Better than good." She leaned over and gave him a quick kiss for emphasis.

"Now don't start that again." He pushed her to arm's length. "About Christmas Eve?"

Oh, right, she'd never given an answer. "Sorry. I was just daydreaming about a kiss beneath the mistletoe."

"I don't think they have those in church."

"Well if they did, more people would attend."

Austin laughed. "You're right about that. So, you'll come with me?"

"I guess I'm available, but after church, we have to find a mistletoe."

"Oh, I think we can make that happen. And a week from then, I need a date for New Year's Eve. You busy?"

"New Year's Eve? Usually." Protesting something stupid like fireworks. "But for you, I'll cancel. Where do you want to go?" Downtown Minneapolis would have some great parties.

"Bowling."

She wrinkled her nose. "Bowling?"

"Yep. Two hours of bowling. All-you-can-eat pizza and all-you-can-drink pop. Plus, prizes and noise makers."

"Whoopee." Rolling her eyes, she twirled a finger beside her head. "You really know how to have fun."

"I do, don't I?"

But it did beat protesting fireworks, and who knew, maybe she and Austin would create their own fireworks when the clock struck midnight.

Oh, yeah.

Or they could do that right now. She started leaning in for another kiss, but he raised his arm and looked at his watch.

"Don't we have some paperwork to fill out?"

She huffed and crossed her arms. "Killjoy."

He grinned. "Been called worse." He gripped one of her arms, pulling it down and then, warming her hand in his, they walked back toward the mall and her car. "Should we go to Bea's or—"

"No, my office is at my mom's place. We'll go there and sign all the paperwork, and then you can kiss me again."

"I have to wait?"

"Yep. Your rules."

"Oh, that's right." He snapped his fingers. "So, you'll drop me off at my place to pick up my car?"

"Actually, that's going in the opposite direction. We'll go to Mom's, sign paperwork, make out a little bit and—"

"Just a little?"

"—and then I'll bring you home because I don't want to get you in trouble with Bea."

"Good plan." He laughed.

It only took twenty minutes to reach her mom's place. In the past, when Dani had brought home a young man, her mom had spouted the no-boyfriends-overnight decree which Dani had more than once ignored.

Another selfish action she'd taken to stoke her mom's ire.

It was no wonder her mom was kicking her out.

She took Austin in through the garage. Her mom's Lexus was there—beside Dani's boxes—so she was home. Dani couldn't wait to tell her that she'd found a place and would be moving this week. And Dani would thank her for booting her out. If not for that, Dani doubted she ever would have grown up. Life would have continued to be all about being in the spotlight and what was best for her.

Even worse, she never would have met Austin, who'd taught

her what selflessness really was.

Now, maybe, she and her mom would have the mother-daughter relationship Dani'd always craved. That would be the best way to begin the New Year.

She took Austin's hand and led him through her mom's home, not surprised to watch his wide eyes take in the enormity of the place.

For one person. Who was away from home far more often than she was here.

Seemed like such a waste when people were sleeping outside on a night like tonight.

But then, how many would choose to leave behind their drugs and alcohol in exchange for the warm bed?

Nope, not going there tonight.

Gripping Austin's hand, she opened the door leading down to the family room. That seemed to be Mom's favorite place to hang out lately. No surprise, she heard voices coming from the television. After sending off paperwork, she would take Austin down there. Mom would be very pleased to see her with him.

In the office, she printed off a real estate purchase agreement which she and Austin signed, turning their verbal agreement into a binding form. He wrote, and griped over, a check for the earnest money deposit. Now their work was done, and it was up to the sellers to sign.

Which meant she got to show off Austin.

She practically dragged him down the steps to the family room. Her bespectacled mom sat on the sectional, huddled over the coffee table covered with paperwork. As usual.

How could her mom stand it? Dani hated the paperwork involved in home selling, but that couldn't compare to politics.

"Mom?" Dani gripped Austin's hand tighter and drew him

closer to her.

Her mom looked up and shook her head, startled, then removed her cheaters. Her gaze flicked from Austin to Dani to their entwined hands and back to their faces. "Austin. How nice to see you again."

"You too, Senator Chamberlain."

She waved her hand. "To you, I'm Felicity." She gestured to the sectional. "Please have a seat. As you can see, I have plenty of room." She tidied up her paperwork and pushed it aside then stood to shake Austin's hand. "I must say, this is a nice surprise." Her gaze flitted to Dani, who grinned.

"I figured you'd be surprised." Dani sat, tugging Austin down with her.

Her mother followed suit. "What brings you two here on this horrible evening?"

"Oh, it wasn't so horrible." Dani glanced at Austin and smirked. His cheeks turned the cutest shade of red.

"I see." Her mom's brows rose.

"It was a huge night." Dani spread out her arms. "I found a place to rent and will be moving in this week, so I'll be out of your hair, and Austin just signed a purchase agreement."

"Wow." Her mom smiled, and it even looked sincere, not that plastic smile she used for the press. "Congratulations to you both. When do you move in, Austin?"

"January thirty-first, and my mom will be moving in a month later."

"What a nice son you are. Where does your mom live now?"

"Mom, that's none—"

"It's okay, Dani." He laid his other hand on top of their folded hands. "It's a fact of my life, and I've learned I can't hide it." Then to her mom he said, "She's been in the Sheridan Correctional

Facility these past seven years and is getting out March first."

Mom just shook her head, her eyes unfocusing. "You never cease to amaze me, young man."

"Just doing what God wants me to."

"If only we could all learn to do that." Her mother looked away as if composing herself, then turned to Austin. "Do you mind my asking what your mother is in for?"

"Mom, really?"

Austin held up his hand. "Honestly, I don't mind. It used to embarrass me, but it's my story. And it helps me break ground with other homeless people. I'm able to meet them where they're at."

Mom squeezed her eyes closed. "And your testimony can convict someone who's hidden too many lies." She shook her head. "Dani's right. It is none of my business."

"Well actually, as you're in politics, maybe you're in a place you can help." Austin let go of Dani's hand and leaned toward her mom. "You see, my mom, like so many others, became addicted to opioids years ago when she hurt her back, and that addiction turned her into something ugly. My grandma shielded my sister and me from a lot of it, but I saw the drug use, her willingness to sell herself. That addiction stole my mom away from me before I had a chance to know her. Too many of the homeless people I talk with at Family Table share the same story, and I'm tired of hearing it."

"You and me both, Austin, you and me both." She connected gazes with Dani. "I promise to do what I can, and I promise that as a mother and wife, not a politician."

"Thank you." He reached for Dani's hand. "And I have another question for you, but I need to be completely forthright to you and Dani before I ask."

"Of course, Austin." Her mom splayed her hands palms open as if ready to receive whatever he had to say.

"Um, it's easy to talk about my mom's sins, but not so much my own." He glanced at Dani then her mom. He told her mom about his past, being homeless, and the family who'd taken him in, despite all that. "Richard and Sheila Brooks showed me mercy I still don't understand. If not for them, I'd likely be in prison, probably would have ended up selling drugs just like my mom. Probably—"

"What?" Dani jerked her hand away. "Selling drugs? That's what your mom was in prison for?"

"Yeah. I thought I'd told you."

She crossed her arms over her chest. "No, I didn't know that your mom was one of the . . . " She eyed her mom and held back a curse word. "Was just like one of the lowlifes who killed my dad. For all I know, she's the one who pulled the trigger."

Mom's eyes grew round as snowballs. "Danielle Chamberlain!"

Suddenly shivering, Dani hugged herself. Her dad had been serving the homeless when he got caught between a drug dealer and the buyer. For all she cared, drug dealers could rot in prison.

"I'm sorry, Dani."

She felt Austin's hand on her arm and shrugged it off. She couldn't look at him. Both her head and her heart told her he had nothing to do with dealing drugs, but he was a reminder of the evil that had stolen her father from her, and she couldn't handle that tonight.

"I'd like you to leave," she spoke barely above a whisper.

"I understand."

She felt the couch cushions lift as he got up.

"Can I call you?" Why did he have to sound so sympathetic?

She shook her head. "I need time."

"Then I'll await your call."

She sat there, unmoving, looking straight ahead, as Austin climbed the stairs. She heard the door open, then shut before a tear trickled down her cheek. Even with an apology, she'd probably just trampled any relationship she wished to have with Austin.

Why couldn't she be levelheaded like her mom? Her uncle? Brother? Austin?

"I'm going to bed." Dani forced herself off the couch and aimed for the steps, her feet shuffling through the plush carpet.

"Good memories live here." Mom's quiet voice forced Dani to stop. Listen for more. "Please, Danielle. It's time you knew the truth."

Truth?

Her jaw and fists clenched, Dani slowly turned toward her mom.

"Mom!" She ran back toward her slumped-over mother, praying like she hadn't prayed in years that her mother hadn't just had another heart attack.

# Chapter Seventeen

*M*om!" Dani slid to her knees on the floor in front of her mother while reaching for her phone. She dropped the phone on the carpet, and it bounced underneath the couch. Her fingers shook as she reached beneath, finally landing on the phone.

"I'm all right, Danielle."

"Uh-uh. I'm calling 911." Danielle punched at the phone but couldn't hit the right numbers.

Her mom laid a hand on hers. "I. Am. Fine."

Dani looked up into her mom's eyes. They were glossed over from tears born of pain. But it wasn't anything she'd dial 911 for.

Her mom patted the cushion beside her. "Please."

Clamping her lips shut, Dani sat near her mom, refusing the offering of a hug. Instead, she wrapped her arms around herself and looked straight ahead at the television airing some Christmas romance with a couple standing beneath a mistletoe.

That could have been—should have been—her and Austin if she had kept her mouth shut.

"Your father kissed me for the first time in this house."

Dani glanced out of the corner of her eye at her mom, refusing to give her the satisfaction of turning her way.

Her mom sighed, shaking her head. "So, so many memories

here. Singing Christmas carols. Baking cookies. So much laughter. And then . . . "

And then a drug dealer took her father's life while he was just trying to help.

"And then drugs took over."

Dani couldn't stop her head from turning her mother's way. "Don't you mean, the drug dealer?"

"No, dear. I mean drugs. They had a hold on your father long before I met him."

Anger knotted every cell in her body. "You're lying."

"I wish I were." Mom folded her hands in her lap, staring off at the family portrait hanging on the wall to their left. "I always thought I could change him. Save him." Her shoulders heaved. "He hated what they turned him into. Hated the control they had over him, yet in the end, he loved them more than us."

"No." Dani shook her head, her mind taking her to a dark place. "He was helping people. That's why he went to the homeless camp."

Her mother sighed again. "That's the spin we put on his story, when the truth was, I kicked him out and told him not to come home until he was clean." She wiped her eyes. "He never came home. A week later, I got the call. No one questioned our story except for the people in the camp, and who believed them?"

"So, you lied to the press? The people who voted you in?" Her stomach churned, and she pressed a hand to her heart. "Me?"

Her mother nodded.

Pain zinged through Dani's chest. Was this what heartbreak felt like? "What about Brad? Does he know?"

Mother nodded again. "He knew about your father's drug abuse and put the pieces together as he got older. That's why he accepted a call so far away. He hated the lies your uncle and I told and needed to get away."

"All so you could stay in politics." Dani spat the word.

"No, no, it was never about politics. It was about preserving your father's name. It was about protecting you. You and your father were so much alike, and you loved him so dearly, I couldn't bring myself to mar the image you had of him. Clearly, I've mucked all of it up."

Her mom sniffled and reached to her left for a tissue. "I'm going to call your uncle and tell him it's time the people knew the truth."

Dani tried to absorb the truth, which churned in her stomach.

Her dad had chosen drugs over her. Over Brad. Over their mom.

He'd chosen homelessness over giving up his addiction.

And she'd told Austin to get out?

She wasn't any better than her mom. Bile scratched its way up her throat. Dani rushed to the bathroom and emptied her stomach before collapsing on the floor. She hugged her arms around her knees and tears spilled for her dad's truth, for the lies she'd been told by people who claimed they loved her, for her brother who couldn't bear to stick around. She couldn't stick around longer either.

Good thing she'd finally found a place to move to. But first, she had to survive two more weeks with her mother. Some Merry Christmas this was going to be.

She gathered her emotions and tucked them away before leaving the bathroom. Her mom sat on the sectional, her legs curled beneath her as she talked on the phone. And she was . . . smiling . . . ?

It didn't compute.

And it didn't matter. Dani was going to reveal her own truth.

Arms crossed, she strode to the couch and stared down at her mom until she ended the call.

Mom set the phone on the coffee table. "You'll be happy to know that your uncle has set up a press conference for tomorrow morning. Minnesota will know the truth. And I'll be resigning."

Dani's arms fell to her sides. "Resigning?" Truth, she expected. "You're not going to fight for your job? You're going to give up serving the people of Minnesota?"

Her mom patted the couch cushion beside her, and Dani obeyed, still keeping a good foot between them.

"Watching you and your young man working your hearts out, not being afraid to interact with people, really being God's hands and feet, has made me realize how little I've achieved over the years. I'm ready to pass the mantle to someone less jaded than I. Someone who still has the fiery passion necessary to affect change. I hope you'll show me how."

A rare tear coursed its way from her mother's eye down her cheek.

Dani grabbed a tissue and wiped her eyes and nose as a realization set in. She wasn't the only one hurting here—she'd been too self-centered to see beyond her own wounds to her mom's heart that was so broken no earthly physician could heal it.

Dani refused to break it further.

She stretched an open hand to her mother who grasped it in a shaky grip. "I'll help you, Mom, if you'll forgive me for all the nasty things I've said to you."

"Sweetheart." Mom wiped a tear from Dani's cheek. "You're already forgiven."

*December 19*

Hi Mom,

Did you get your Christmas gift? I remember from when we all lived with Grandma that you liked to read. Guess that's where I got it from. Anyway, hope you still like books.

How do you spend your Christmas there? Do you get good food? What about a church service?

I found a house last night, and I move in the end of January! It'll be perfect for us, and there'll be space when Brittany visits too. The whole house needs to be painted, but that's easy. Do you have a favorite color I can paint your bedroom? It should be done by the time you come home.

Home.

I want this to be your home too, Mom. I do. I can't wait until you come home! Never ever thought I'd say that, but I mean it.

Um, besides looking for houses, something else happened last night . . .

That woman I told you about, the one I sort of liked? Okay, not sort of, but really, really liked. Well, turns out she sort of liked me. Or so I thought . . .

Confused? Yeah, me too.

*She kissed me last night. Is that something I'm supposed to tell my mom? I don't know, so if I'm breaking mother/son protocol, oh well.*

*Anyway, she kissed me, or I kissed her. I don't remember who made the first move, but I do know it was a mutual attraction. She was going to spend Christmas with me.*

*I was thinking for the first time ever I'd have someone to ring in the New Year with. Maybe more.*

*And then . . .*

*Then it all fell apart.*

*She learned what you were in for and freaked out as if I had something to do with it, and now I don't know where we stand.*

*To be honest, if that's the way she's gonna be, I don't know that I want anything to do with her. She's impulsive and she overreacts, and I've got enough drama in my life already without the queen of drama queens adding to it, right?*

*So, I get to spend Christmas alone, and New Year's Eve. It never bothered me before.*

*Does a broken heart ever mend? Cause it sure hurts right now.*

*I'm probably best off on my own, like I always thought. Besides, you'll be home soon, right? So, I won't really be alone.*

*I hope I can be a good son to you.*

*Anyway, see you soon.*

*Love,*

*Austin*

*December 25*

> *"For unto you is born this day*
> *in the city of David a Savior,*
> *who is Christ the Lord.*
> *And this will be a sign for you:*
> *you will find a baby*
> *wrapped in swaddling cloths*
> *and lying in a manger."*

*Hi Mom,*

*Today we celebrated Jesus' birth. I believe He was born to save us. So does Brittany. Grandma did too. Do you?*

*Sometimes I think, 'What if Jesus was born today instead of 2000 years ago?' Where would He have been born? Could easily have been one of the homeless communities I serve. When I think about the King of the Universe being born there, it gives me goosebumps. He really did come to serve.*

*So, I couldn't think of a better way to spend the day than by serving at the Family Table Meal. I try to see the person Jesus sees in each face, in each heart. It's not easy. But you know who makes it look easy?*

*Dani.*

*Yeah, the ~~girl~~ woman I like. She was there today (with her mom and uncle) and last week too. She even apologized last week for freaking out on me. And my response? Uh, duh, duh. Each time I try to talk to her, my brain short circuits and forgets how to send words to my mouth. She's gonna think I don't care anymore. But I do. More every week, it seems. Maybe I'm afraid of being abandoned again, so I'm doing the abandoning. Stupid, right?*

*She treats everyone like they're her best friend. Even those who claim they want to be left alone. She looks them in the eye and smiles and laughs or cries. She touches those who allow it, who need it, and seems to know the difference between those who need touch and those who would recoil. Yeah, she can be impulsive, but that also shows her heart, her passion.*

*Am I making excuses for her? Maybe. I don't know.*

*I do know I need to talk with her. Hopefully before my next letter to you.*

*Anyway, hope you had a good Christmas. We'll make sure next year's celebration will be the best ever.*

*Love,*
*Austin*

## Chapter Eighteen

"That goes in the master bedroom." Dani directed the mover carrying a lamp. If she weren't such a drama queen, such a spoiled-rotten diva, Austin would be here with her today, helping, and celebrating her true move to independence. On New Year's Eve, of all days, and ringing in the new year with a memorable kiss.

Today was memorable all right. Her first New Year's Eve spent alone. Mom was enjoying her newfound freedom by flying to Kansas City to celebrate with Brad. Uncle Harris and Aunt Helen were off in some exotic place.

And she was schlepping boxes.

This was what she got for putting her dad on a pedestal. Talk about misplaced passions! She was lucky her mom hadn't kicked her to the curb a week and a half ago when Dani had gone ballistic on Austin.

Who was now giving her the silent treatment, and it hurt like crazy. No wonder her loved ones hated it coming from her. That was a childish tactic she needed to lock away forever.

She walked up the steps to her new bedroom, now filled with a bed and boxes with stuff that had no real meaning.

Why did Austin, the one who opened her eyes to what serving really meant, have to be a casualty of her idiocy?

She'd texted apologies several times. Asked how he was doing. Wished him Merry Christmas. Exchanged shallow pleasantries at the Family Table Meal on Christmas Day. Told him she would still love to go bowling tonight. Yet all she heard back was crickets.

With noon's sunlight streaming through her window, she lay down on her unmade mattress, took out her cellphone, and checked it for the twentieth time today, probably more. No message back from Austin.

A mover appeared in her doorway. "That's all of it, Ms. Chamberlain."

Already? She leapt from her bed. "Thank you," she told his back as he turned away. She looked around the room for her purse. Where had she left it?

*The kitchen. That's right.*

She hurried down the steps and asked the movers to wait a second. She located her purse on the kitchen counter, right where she'd left it. Good thing she'd employed honest men. Any of the three guys working could have taken her handbag.

From her wallet, she took out three hundred-dollar bills and handed one each to the movers, eliciting grins she hadn't seen once during the move. "Thank you for your help. Have a happy new year."

"Thank you, Ms. Chamberlain. Enjoy your new year in your home."

"I will." She lied. "Thank you."

And they walked out into the blustery winter leaving her alone in her new home.

A new home with no one to celebrate with.

Not her mom.

Not her brother.

Not her loony activist friends.

Not Austin.

All her life she'd done what she could to be noticed, to avoid being alone. Abandoned. Forgotten like those spending the night without a home or food.

Yet here she was.

Alone.

*That's enough, Danielle!* She strode from the kitchen. No more feeling sorry for herself. She should be grateful. She had a warm home and plenty of food. And she did have family who loved her, in spite of herself.

She flicked on the gas fireplace, selected the Christmas music list on her phone's Spotify app, and headed back to the kitchen where she attached her phone to mini speakers. No one needed to be with her to celebrate. Making this place a home would be ample celebration. She started in the kitchen by emptying boxes and filling her cupboards. She moved to the bathroom, then the living room, her office, and finally, with the sun long set, she aimed for her bedroom. She turned on the TV and listened to New Year countdowns while emptying boxes and cozying up the room.

An hour later, she had one box to go.

A heavy box full of books that should have been marked for her office. Well, she'd carry the books there by the handful rather than break her back by hefting the too-full box.

She slit it open, lifted the flaps, and stopped.

At the very top was her dad's Bible, the one he used to read to her from, back when she'd thought he was the perfect father.

With tears threatening, Dani removed the Bible from the box. Clutching it to her chest, she crawled onto her newly-made bed. She wasn't alone—she had a piece of her dad. She reclined against the pillows lined up along her headboard and brought the Bible to her nose hoping for some hint of her father.

But time had worn away any sensory memories.

She opened the book and turned the thin pages to the Psalms, many highlighted in yellow. Alongside many of King David's laments, her father had penned his own laments about letting his family down and not being able to kick his addiction. How much he loved her mom and Brad and herself. He struggled with worthlessness and loneliness.

She paged through more of the Bible. One of the first verses he'd underlined from Genesis was: "'It is not good that the man should be alone: I will make him a helper fit for him.'" Beside that he wrote, *and God gifted me with Felicity.*

In Deuteronomy he underlined, "' . . . he will never leave you nor forsake you.'"

Then Psalm 73 said, "I am continually with you; you hold my right hand."

And Matthew 28 promised, "'Behold, I am with you always, to the end of the age.'"

Her father had outlined so many more verses promising that God was with him even in his brokenness. Always. And He didn't want people to be alone. Beside many of those, her dad wrote a single word, *Hope.*

Dani slapped shut the book, sat up straight, and looked upward, anger building inside. "Really? Dad was hopeful? You don't want us to be alone? Then why did he find solace in drugs? Huh? Where is my hope? And why do I hate being alone? I've been seeking attention my entire life. Where have you been?"

*Have you sought that attention from Me?*

Whoa.

She fell back against the pillows.

Was that it? Had she been seeking attention in the wrong places? From her mom. From the press. From Austin. Even from Sammi.

She didn't have a heart for the homeless. No, she wanted to be seen having that heart.

Suddenly her mom's and uncle's silence when it came to their service made sense. They weren't doing it for glory or to make the news. They were simply serving out of love. If they'd told others, then their actions would have been self-serving rather than pointing to God and giving Him the glory, letting Him work in people's hearts.

Like He was doing with hers at this very moment.

That was what Mom and Uncle Harris had told her. What Brad had preached to her. What Austin had demonstrated.

She'd even read those verses in the Bible before, but they hadn't ever spoken to her heart like this.

Not until now.

Shame forced her prostrate on the bed. "I have been selfish, and I've been seeking attention from all the wrong things, all the wrong people. Can You forgive me? Can You change my heart so that it seeks You and no one else?"

Dani lay like that, silent, until the countdown on the television broke through.

Four . . . Three . . . Two . . . One . . .

"Happy New Year!" Dani called out with the TV announcers.

It was going to be a happy new year.

On Saturday, she'd see Austin at the Family Table Meal and tell him.

*January 1*

*Happy New Year, Mom!*

*And before you even ask, no I have not spoken with Dani yet. I'm chicken. She sends me texts, but I don't respond, telling myself I'd rather talk in person. But do I make the effort to meet with her?*

*No.*

*As I said, I'm chicken. Relationships are scary— they always seem to end with someone leaving me behind.*

*I did think about her last night during the countdown, though . . .*

*Maybe she's worth the risk of being left.*

*Since I'd found my home, my schedule opened up and I was able to fly to New York for a few days. I spent time with friends there who—guess what?— told me I needed to put on my big boy pants and talk to her. So, I will. I promise. She chiseled out this place in my heart shaped just for her and it physically hurts not seeing her, talking with her.*

*Is that love?*

*This Saturday I'm working the Family Table Meal and hopefully she'll be there. I won't let her leave without saying something to her, even if I have to* write it all down on paper in advance.

Surprisingly, I've learned writing is a good way to process my feelings. Thank you for listening.

You have been reading my letters, right? I'd love to hear back from you.

Just think, in a couple of months, you get to come home. I still don't know what color you want your room. I want to make it as homey for you as possible.

See you soon,

Love,

Austin

# Chapter Nineteen

The silent treatment from Austin now expanded to three weeks, and Dani couldn't take it anymore. Before she left today, they were going to have a conversation, even if that conversation was about setting a time for a heart-to-broken heart . When it came to love, nothing hurt worse than being ignored.

And yeah, she'd fallen fast and hard for one Austin Lang, and she needed to tell him what her heart felt.

She carried dirty plates back to the Family Table kitchen and cast a glance at Austin in his element at the stove, flipping pancakes. From what she gleaned from the diners, they were the best pancakes ever. She wouldn't find out, though. With Austin keeping their conversations at a professional level, she'd lost her appetite and it wouldn't return until she could tell him about the changes in her heart.

And that she'd given up her activism. Instead she was taking a crochet class with her mom, so they could make hats and scarves and blankets to bring to the homeless and make a life-changing difference. Yeah, her protests had focused attention on the homeless, but they'd also drawn attention to her.

And she was no longer okay with that.

She set the dirty dishes in a container outside the kitchen and snuck another glance at Austin.

Well, a little attention from him wouldn't hurt.

She walked around the hall, talking with the diners, keeping an eye out for Sammi who had yet to show up. Last week she'd had an awful cough.

*She's okay, isn't she God?*

Dani didn't like the silent answer.

She served and cleaned several more rounds of pancakes with no sign of Sammi. That just wouldn't suffice. Dani needed to know she was okay because her churning gut told her otherwise.

And she could not do nothing.

Maybe Austin knew where she was.

After the final diner left, she cleared the last of the dishes and dug her community service sheet out of her pocket. She'd put in about forty hours so far which meant she'd still get to see Austin for another twelve Saturdays or so. Those Saturdays would be much easier to face if they were on speaking terms.

She looked around the room for him—to ask about Sammi and to set a time for their talk. Hopefully tonight would work. She needed to see his smile again, and hear his laugh, both of which she'd stolen.

He wasn't in the kitchen, which was unusual, but at a table with other volunteers.

Laughing.

Well, at least she hadn't stolen his laugh completely.

Forcing her lips into a smile, dreading the business-only encounter, she carried her sheet to the table and stood across from Austin. "Have a moment?" She held up her form.

He startled and looked up at her. A smile flashed across his face then disappeared completely.

"Sure." He reached for the form.

"No, I mean, can I have a word with you?"

"Oh. Sure. Excuse us for a moment," he told those at the table and joined Dani by the kitchen pass-through, his hands stuck so far in his pockets, Captain America would have trouble pulling them out. "Is something wrong?"

She wanted to say, "Yeah, us not being together is wrong." But this wasn't the place for a personal conversation. For now, she pointed to the corner of the room where Sammi usually sat by herself. "I didn't see Sammi today, and she was really sick last week. Do you have any idea where she might be, uh, living?" If that was what it was called.

"Sammi?"

Dani shrugged. "Well, that's the name I gave her since she wouldn't tell me who she was."

He actually laughed. "Why am I not surprised?" Then his smile faded. "Could you describe her?"

"Probably a few years older than us. I'm guessing about five foot two, five three. I think her hair is brown. Shoulder length. Always wears that long trench coat. Sound familiar?"

He stared off toward the corner, his eyes glazing over, and he shook his head. "Yeah, I know who you're talking about. Always keeps to herself. Says nothing but 'Get lost.'"

"Yeah, that's her."

He shrugged. "I don't know where she goes from here, but chances are she's sleeping in the tent city."

"I think she's sick."

"A lot of these people are sick."

"She needs attention."

"Dani, she knows where to go if she's sick."

"I know that." All diners were given information on where to go for help. "But that doesn't mean she went."

He sighed. "It's not up to you to save her."

"What if she's alone?" Dani sniffled. "Do you know how cold it is out there? My fingers froze in my lined gloves just walking from my car."

"There are people out there helping."

"But Sammi hides. They won't see her."

Austin somehow managed to drag his hands from his pockets and wrapped her in a hug. "You can pray for her."

"Yeah. That's what I'll do." That and more. She shrugged out of Austin's arms and wiped her nose.

"Actually, Dani."

"One more thing." They spoke at the same time, so Dani motioned for Austin to go first.

He stuck his hand in his pocket and pulled out a piece of paper. "There's something I want to—"

"Austin, what do we do with this?"

He turned toward the kitchen where two people were hefting a griddle. He sighed and muttered something to himself while sticking the note back into his pocket, then called out, "Be right with you." He touched Dani's arm, and his gaze met hers, making her insides warm as chicken soup. "Call me, okay?"

"Tonight?"

"I'd like that." Then he took off for the kitchen.

She would call him tonight after she learned what happened to Sammi. No way was she going to let that woman be by herself. Nothing was worse than being sick alone, having no one to bring you chicken noodle soup or hot cocoa or your favorite stuffed animal. All of which her mom had always done. Her mom had been there for her all her life, and yet Dani had shoved that love aside hoping for her dad. More evidence of her selfishness.

She would not let Sammi be alone.

Even if that meant going to the tent city all by herself.

Austin helped the volunteers find a home for all the kitchen gear and then looked around for Dani. Everyone had left. Including her.

Rats. He felt for the note in his pocket. Still there.

When he got home, he'd give her a call. Maybe they could meet for pizza or something tonight.

In the meantime, though, he sat at a table and pulled a different letter out of his pocket, one the mail carrier had delivered right before Austin came today. One he hadn't had time to read but had kept him on edge all morning and early afternoon.

A letter from his mom.

With trembling fingers, he slit open the envelope, pulled out the lined piece of paper, and read.

> *My Dear Austin,*
>
> *Can I still call you that? I know my "mom" credentials are about as low as they come, but your letters have changed me. Really, they have!*
>
> *I'm sorry I haven't written back. To be honest, I haven't felt worthy of the love you've shown me. But I'm learning to see that God even loves drug addicts like me.*
>
> *I've been clean for seven years now, but it's been pretty easy in here. Being free again scares me. I don't want to be the person I was when I was sentenced. I want to be who I was before drugs took*

*over my life and became my god. I want to know the God you've told me about. The one your grandma praised. The one our chaplain preaches about.*

*Will you pray for me? Please?*

*As for your broken heart . . .*

*I'm certainly not the one to ask. My relationships were all too shallow for the heart to be affected, so maybe the fact that your heart is breaking is a good thing. It shows that you know how to love and are willing to risk being hurt.*

*Perhaps that addresses what you said in a previous letter, that you're meant to be alone. Take the risk again, Austin, please. One thing I've learned from the chaplain here is that the Potter (God) takes broken vessels—like you and me—and fixes them up into something beautiful. So, yeah, you have a broken heart, but let God mend it, okay?*

*Ha ha. Here I am giving you a sermon. I know, funny, right?*

*Anyway, I do love you, Austin. You and Brittany. And I can't wait to see you again. I promise I'll try harder. I promise. I want to re-earn that title of Mom.*

*Love,*

*Your . . . mom.*

*P.S. Yellow is my favorite color. The color of sunlight.*

Austin sniffled and wiped a hand across his nose. Yes, yes! he'd pray for her! Had been praying for years. His perseverance was paying off, thank you, God. Maybe her living with him wouldn't be so bad. Maybe a real relationship would be birthed.

He'd have to keep praying about that too.

He couldn't wait to tell Dani about the letter.

*Dani.*

Yeah, she'd broken his heart, but then he'd been just as much of a drama queen by ignoring her. *Real mature, Lang.* Love really did make you do stupid things.

He had to call her. Invite her to pizza tonight. Maybe both of them could act like mature adults, and he'd read his letter to her telling her how he really felt, that his feelings had whooshed right past crush and he'd fallen hard into love. He pulled out his phone and pressed her number.

No answer, which was unusual for her. Needing to be available for clients at a moment's notice, she always answered.

Or maybe she was ignoring him as he'd ignored her.

Something niggled at the thought of her name, but it wasn't just longing. It was fear.

She wouldn't go to that tent city all alone to find Sammi, would she? After all their warnings to go with a group?

Ha. This was Dani he was thinking about. Impulsive. Reckless. Huge-hearted Dani who would risk herself to help someone else.

He hurried around the fellowship hall, shutting off all the lights in the church, locking all the doors, and then he ran toward his car. His toe caught on a crack in the sidewalk, and he flew face first toward the ground. His knee crashed into ice-covered concrete. Stifling a curse, he pushed up and limped to his car. He started it up and turned on the heater full blast. Before taking off, he called Dani's uncle and asked to meet him down at the homeless camp. Unlike Dani, Austin knew not to go alone, and Dani's uncle had a lot of connections.

Austin prayed as he pulled onto the street and quickly surpassed the speed limit.

"God, help me get there safely, but more importantly, please keep Dani safe."

Goosebumps broke out over Dani's body as she walked through the tent city, and not because of the freezing temperatures. Before when she'd come here, she'd been with others and hadn't looked, really looked at the people living in flimsy tents in January in Minnesota. Some had fires going inside their tents in spite of the fact that fires had broken out here several times in the past month. She supposed that was the risk they took to stay warm.

Knowing what she did about Sammi, she looked for a tent or dwelling apart from the rest. Every few feet, she cuffed her hands around her mouth and yelled out, "Sammi" with no answer.

The door of a tent ahead of her opened and a huge, red-bearded man stepped out. "You lookin' for someone?"

Dani clutched the mace in her hand and raised her chin, hoping to show confidence. "A woman about five two, brown hair. Wears a super-huge trench coat."

He smiled. Or was it a sneer? Regardless, it sent shivers down her spine. "Oh, you mean Daphne."

Daphne? That sure didn't fit the woman she knew. Or tried to know. But if this man knew her . . . She clutched her mace tighter, flipping the safety latch. "Yeah, Daphne. You know where she is?"

"Yeah." He pointed to a tent behind the one he came out of. It was hidden, exactly the type of location Sammi would prefer.

"Right back there. Let me show you." Something glinted in his eyes and made her stomach turn flip flops. Was that her gut warning her away? Or just stupid fear?

For Sammi, she had to risk it.

She headed for the tent and felt the big man's presence right behind her. Then she felt his breath on her neck, sending chills down her spine. She started raising her hand with the mace, and he slapped her hand, sending the mace who knew where. His massive hands gripped her shoulders and pushed her into the tent. She opened her mouth to scream but a filthy cloth was stuffed inside it. She tried kicking, flailing while someone else held down her legs and arms.

Redbeard ripped off her coat, shredding the zipper and her last remnant of safety.

*Oh, Lord, help me!*

## Chapter Twenty

*A*ustin cuffed his hands over his mouth and called, "Dani!" Behind him, Dani's uncle and some police officers he'd enlisted were doing the same.

She was here. Her car sat a block away from the tents. Windows were broken. Tires and radio and more removed.

What had she been thinking coming down here alone?

Why hadn't he listened to her when she asked for help?

"Lookin' for your girlfriend?" a voice spoke behind him.

Fear clenching his heart, Austin wheeled and looked at the woman in the long trench coat. Sammi.

"Have you seen her?" he asked, afraid to hear the answer.

"Over there." She pointed toward the back of the city. "Behind the big tent."

"Thanks." Austin started that way then stopped. He wouldn't be any better than Dani if he took off without a backup. He whistled to get her uncle's and officers' attention then gestured toward the tent hidden behind a barricade of others, a perfect place to hide trouble.

They ran toward him and he took off.

And tripped over a rut on the ground, re-scraping his already sore knee.

"You okay?" Uncle Harris lifted him up. "You sure she's in there?"

"No, but a . . . a friend of Dani's said she was there."

"Don't go in." One of the officers pushed him aside. "We've got this."

"But—" Austin stretched toward the tent door, but Uncle Harris held him back as the officers rushed to the tent, hollered out a warning, then bolted inside.

"Son, I'm as scared as you are, but they do their job best without interference."

"What if . . . ?" He'd heard horror stories of what some people did down here. If Dani was hurt, he'd never forgive himself.

"Pray."

Oh, he was, but with his eyes wide open.

A second later, Dani rushed from the tent. Her gaze landed on him and she ran toward him, crying, tucking her coat tight around her body.

He rushed to her, trying to ignore the pain screaming from his knee, his arms open to receive her.

She ran into his arms and burrowed her face in his jacket. "I thought they . . . " Her voice quivered.

"Shhh. You're safe now." He kissed her forehead and cradled her head against his chest.

"And a fool. I put myself—"

"Stop it." He pulled back, but she kept a tight grip on him. "Are you okay to walk?"

She nodded, tears dropping off her chin. "But . . . but the police don't want me to leave. They want me to give a statement."

"Then we all stay." He wrapped an arm around her, hoping to warm away her shakes, and whispered in her ear. "I won't let the woman I love be hurt again."

Her head slowly turned to him until their gazes met. "The woman you love?"

"Not exactly how I wanted to tell you, but yeah. I've just been too stupid to tell you."

"Well then I guess we make a perfect pair." She snuggled into his arms and Austin breathed in the fruity scent of her hair mixed with the sweat of fear. "For the record, I love you, too."

"You—"

"Here's a blanket for her."

Sammi? Keeping an arm around Dani, Austin turned to the woman Dani had come out here to find.

She handed him what looked like a newly-knitted blanket.

"Thank you, Sammi." He wrapped the blanket around Dani.

"Whatever." The woman shrugged. "And it's Cherise. My name's Cherise."

*January 8*

*Hi Mom,*

 *Got your letter on Saturday. It was so good hearing from you! And yellow, it is.*

 *Saturday was quite the day.*

 *I got your letter but couldn't read it until after the Family Table Meal. I meant to read Dani a letter I'd written her, but she pulled a typical Dani stunt and went to save someone at the homeless camp. Big surprise, Dani was the one who needed saving.*

 *She gives my heart so many jumpstarts!*

 *But that is good.*

 *It's hard to keep your feelings buried when the person you love is in danger. Yeah, I love her, and I told her so. Miracle of miracles, she feels the same way!*

 *I think she might be the one, Mom. Is this too quick? All I know is that she adds a spark to my life, and I think I help ground her. Her mom and aunt and uncle really like me too.*

 *Dani and I spent the last two days making up for all the non-talking (and non-kissing) we'd been doing. Is that too much information?*

 *Well, gotta say goodbye. I gave my students*

*homework over Christmas break, so now I get to spend my evening correcting that homework.*

*Just think, I'll see you in a month and a half! I'll be waiting for you outside those prison gates, and you get to come home to a yellow room.*

*Love you,*

*Austin*

# Chapter Twenty-One

This was not the Valentine's Day Dani had imagined, but if she'd read the vibes Austin had given off correctly, this was going to be a day to remember. Yeah, they'd only known each other less than three months, had been going out far less than that, but she was ready to make their relationship permanent.

Her brother would roll his eyes and call her impulsive.

She'd just smile back at him and say, "Yep, and happy to be who God made me to be." As long as she avoided running into dangerous situations. She shivered at the remembrance of Redbeard's hands ripping off her jacket. Austin had saved her from herself, and she could spend the rest of her life thanking him.

She made one last swipe of the paintbrush on the wall of the bedroom that would belong to Austin's mom. She stood back to admire the sunny yellow, while the tantalizing aroma of Crock-Pot roast beef wafted toward her from the kitchen. Her stomach replied. Loudly.

Thank goodness Austin wasn't in here to hear that. He'd have a good laugh at her expense. Well, maybe that wasn't such a bad thing after all.

She set the paintbrush in the bucket of paint supplies and

sighed as loudly as her stomach begged for food. At last Austin's home was finished. Two weeks of scrubbing tiles and grout, removing layers of wallpaper, tugging up carpet that had stains she didn't want to know what had made them.

And then came the painting of every room.

Yellow for Austin's mom because it reminded her of the sun which she'd seen little of the last seven years. The rest of the house was white with accents of slate blue. Not what Dani would have chosen, but it fit Austin.

Hopefully, this room would satisfy his mother.

With one last look, she picked up the bucket and carried it carefully across the newly sanded and stained hardwood floors to the basement which wasn't nearly as creepy as it had seemed a month and a half ago.

Getting rid of cobwebs definitely helped. Austin had even spread out some carpet remnants and set up a gaming area.

She set the supply bucket on a workbench and wrapped the wet brush in plastic wrap to clean later, after the Valentine's Day meal she and Austin would be sharing with her mom and Bea, who had invited themselves.

Austin had been too nice to tell them "Absolutely not!"

If she had her way, they would not be staying long.

She hurried up the stairs to the kitchen where Austin was slicing and peeling potatoes with the help of Bea, and her mom was throwing together a salad. Dani had chosen the right chore for today. She could wield a paint brush with far more skill than she could handle cooking utensils.

"Hey there." She swept into the kitchen, squeezing past her mom and Bea to Austin and pressed a kiss to his cheek. "Can I take a few minutes to shower?"

"You look perfect."

She raised her paint-splattered hands and arms. "I don't think so." If he thought she would be proposed to while wearing grubbies and being covered in paint, he was kidding himself. "Give me fifteen minutes."

"Make that thirty." Her mom laughed at her own joke.

"Ha ha." Dani retrieved her luggage bag from Austin's room and hurried to the tiny bathroom. It took her five minutes alone to get out all her shower and beauty supplies. Thirty minutes 'til supper was probably accurate. Oh, she hated her mom being right.

Still she showered as quickly as she could and then made herself Instagram presentable.

Now for supper.

She packed her bag, stored it in Austin's room, then hurried to the dining room and sat at the open seat. The food looked delicious, but how could it be anything else with Austin preparing it? The table was set with a mishmash of dishes. Last week he'd mused about getting a matching set, but she'd talked him out of it. This was who he and she were: broken people molded together by the Master Potter to form a beautiful new creation.

Well, that was what she dreamed of for the very near future.

If Austin intended to propose, would he do it with Bea and her mom around? She hoped not. Yeah, she loved her mom, but no way could she give Austin a Valentine's Day kiss to remember with her mom lurking.

Austin reached for her and Bea's hands and soon they were all connected. He gave thanks for the meal and for the people sharing it with him and for his home and his mom who would be moving in soon.

That would be . . . interesting.

Regardless, this was home. So different from the sterile apartment she'd lived in for the past couple years. So different from her mom's place and even Dani's new place. It was home another way. True home was all about letting go of your selfish needs and serving, loving others.

As Austin loved on the homeless.

As Bea loved those she took into her home. A young woman had already moved into Austin's old apartment.

As Mom had loved her constituents enough to tell the truth. They'd begged her not to resign, but she knew it was time. Now she was learning new ways to love others.

They said "Amen" and dug into the food. With Austin's cooking, she would have to double her efforts to stay slim.

"So, tell me." Her mom set down her fork in between bites and during conversation, a new habit since her heart attack. "What have you heard from Sammi-slash-Cherise?"

A subject she'd gladly talk about. Cherise had stepped out of her comfort zone to save Dani, and Dani quickly returned the favor. "We finally talked her into going to New Foundation, a faith-based recovery center for people dealing with alcohol and/or drug addiction. She still doesn't talk much, but she did tell me her ex-husband and kids were supporting her. I'm praying she follows through. Alcohol really has a grip on her."

"As drugs tend to do." Her mom wiped her nose with her napkin, a sign to Dani that she was trying not to cry. "I'll be praying too."

"Thank you." Dani nodded to her mother.

They shared more small talk as the meal dragged on, not that she wasn't enjoying the time with everyone, but it was Valentine's Day. She wanted time alone with Austin. Go ahead, call her selfish.

Austin's phone chirped out a tune from the kitchen counter. It stopped. And then it chirped again.

"Uh-oh." He got up quickly. "That's the trouble signal."

"Trouble?" Dani pushed away from the table and joined him in the kitchen.

"Um, yeah." He kept his face angled away from her as the phone chirped one more time. This time he answered, "This is Austin."

She tried to discern what the caller was saying, but they talked too softly. And Austin just replied with several uh-huhs and uh-ohs and even an *uff da* before hanging up.

"I've gotta go." Still avoiding looking at her, he hurried to the entry closet and pulled out his jacket.

"I'm coming with you." No way was she spending Valentine's Day without him.

"Dani." He zipped his coat and looked back at her, giving her the can't-you-for-once-just-listen look.

To which she crossed her arms. "I can help."

"You don't know what you're getting yourself into. A bunch of people have broken into the church demanding a Valentine's Day meal."

Dani blinked. Imagined all the hungry people out there, lonely people who just wanted someone to see them. Love them. She raised her chin. "Then I recommend we serve them." She gave Austin a shove. "What are you waiting for?"

"You're gonna drive me crazy."

"My life goal."

Twenty-five minutes, a brief stop at a florist to pick up whatever flowers they had left, and a whole bunch of figuring-out-where-they-were-going-to-get-food later they were at the lit-up church where the Family Table Meal was usually served. Her mom had called in a bunch of favors and restaurants "gladly" donated food, desserts, beverages. Mom and Bea would join them to help serve and they'd called in other volunteers to help.

Dani had anticipated a Valentine's Day to remember, though this was not the one she'd dreamt of.

She helped Austin lug the flowers into the church and down to the fellowship hall where they served.

Her jaw dropped, and she jerked to a stop right inside the doorway, trying to get a grip on what she was seeing.

Oh, the basement was loaded with diners all right, but they were already being served, by volunteers, the same meal Austin had made back at his home. The kitchen was also full of people cooking and cleaning.

Her mom and Bea were right in the middle of it, as were Richard and his wife, and Uncle Harris and Aunt Helen.

Speechless, her mouth still hanging open, Dani slowly turned to Austin while strangers took the flowers from them.

He grinned and took her hand. "Come here." He led her to the front of the room, up on a stage where a pulpit usually stood. He leaned over and whispered in her ear. "I've never heard you so quiet."

"What's going on?" she whispered back as he got down on a knee.

Here? She slapped a hand to her chest and with wide eyes, stared down at Austin. In front of all these people?

Austin took her other hand and someone—her eyes were too blurry to discern who—stuck a microphone in front of his mouth.

Seriously? Her quiet, anti-attention seeker boyfriend was going to broadcast his proposal to this entire room of people?

Made her love him even more. She fluttered a hand in front of her face, as if that would stop the tears.

"Richard told me that when I found the right person, I'd know it, and that when I knew it, I shouldn't wait." He pulled a crumpled piece of paper from a pocket and straightened it out. "I've been wanting to read this to you for weeks. Figured now was a good time."

And he'd rendered her speechless. Someone pressed a tissue into her hand, and she wiped her eyes.

Austin held the paper in front of him but kept his gaze on her. "Dani, I had a crush on you from the moment you breezed into this church with your designer handbag and clothes. And then when you, without hesitation, leaped in to help people, that crush went a whole lot deeper. You add spice, flavor to my life. I love the way you love. And I love the way you pull me out of my don't-want-attention place."

"Austin . . . " She cupped a hand on his cheek. "I—"

"Shhhh." He put a finger to her lips.

Oh, the man was going to drive her crazy, making her hold in her love for him.

He folded up the note, tucked it into his pocket, then took her other, trembling hand. "Dani, I adore the joy you've found with Jesus. You make me smile and laugh, and I can't imagine my life anymore without you in it. I hope you feel the same way."

"You know I do, Austin Lang. You've taught me what it really means to love."

He puffed out a breath, and perspiration beaded on his forehead.

If he didn't ask the question soon, he was going to faint right in front of everyone.

She whispered into the microphone, "Are you going to ask the question or not?"

"What question?" He grinned. "I just wanted to read this

letter to you."

Laughter echoed around the room.

"Oh, you think you're so funny." If that was how he was going to be, she had to take matters into her own hands. She grabbed the microphone and held it close to her lips. "Austin Lang." She looked down at his amused face. "Will you marry me?"

His eyes grew big as the buns they were serving tonight, and his mouth dropped open.

"Well?" She grinned and tugged his hand, prompting him to stand.

He returned her grin and spoke softly in her ear. "You have to take over the show, don't you?"

"You just said you loved that about me."

"And I do."

"Is that a yes?" She spoke into the mic.

"That's an absolutely, yes."

With all the onlookers cheering, she gave him a chaste, G-rated kiss.

"Come on, Danielle." Her mother's voice broke through the cheers. "You've just gotten engaged, kiss the man."

And so, she did.

Who was she to disobey her mother?

*Dear Reader,*

*Thank you for reading Dani and Austin's story! These two young people opened my eyes to what being God's hands and feet really looks like. They showed me what it means to serve and challenged me to do a better job of seeing and serving those in need.*

*If you enjoyed* **Home Another Way***, please consider sharing a book review on Amazon, telling other readers why you liked this story. The review doesn't have to be long or eloquent, just honest.*

*You'll find further inspiration and encouragement at http://pottershousebooks.com/ and by reading other books in this uplifting series. Find all the books on Amazon and on The Potter's House Books website.*

*To be notified of all my new releases, join my email list at BrendaAndersonBooks.com/Subscribe. As a Thank You for subscribing, you will receive a FREE copy of* **Coming Home***, a Coming Home Series short story.*

*Thank you for joining me on this writing journey!*

*In Him,*

*Brenda*

## Acknowledgements

Thank you to the six other Potter's House Books authors who've all shared beautiful stories of God molding people's lives. It's been an honor writing alongside all of you!

Thanks also goes to:

My Book Booster Team ~ for tirelessly spreading the word about my books!

Robin from my fabulous church, The Crux ~ You have such a beautiful heart for the homeless! Thank you for sharing your valuable insight into homeless communities.

Joseph Courtemanche, AKA Santa Joe ~ for being the inspiration behind Austin's work with the Family Table Meal. You truly model what it means to be Jesus' hands and feet.

Stacy Monson ~ for helping me reshape this story. Without your wisdom, this story was a mess!

Lesley Ann McDaniel ~ for once again helping to make my stories shine!

Gayle Balster ~ for reading a horrible early draft and offering encouragement!

Sarah, Bryan, and Brandon ~ I love seeing how each of you are serving in your own ways!

My husband, Marvin ~ Your continued encouragement and cheerleading gives me the push I need every day to keep writing. Without you, I'd have quit long ago.

And thank you, Jesus, the Mighty King who came to serve. To you alone be the glory!

Other Potter's House Books
By Brenda S. Anderson

*Long Way Home*

*Place Called Home*

*Home Another Way*

Other Books by Brenda S. Anderson

## Find all of Brenda S. Anderson's books at:
www.BrendaAndersonBooks.com/books

### *Coming Home Series*

## Praise for the Coming Home Series

"Anderson tackles family dynamics, tough issues, and gritty realism in her Coming Home series. From special needs babies to abortion and homelessness, you'll root for her authentic characters as they face real life struggles."

— Award-winning author, **Shannon Taylor Vannatter**

" . . . heartfelt, heart-wrenching fiction at its best, exploring relationships and family, love, faith and forgiveness in fresh, life-changing ways. I see myself in these endearing, enduring characters, their weaknesses and struggles and hard-won triumphs."

— **Laura Frantz**, author of *A Moonbow Night*

"Anderson thrusts her readers into the gritty underbelly of family life and she doesn't mince words or shy away from the difficulties that complicate relationships. The reoccurring themes of grace and restitution are delivered with heart-wrenching honesty. These compelling stories celebrate the joys and sorrows of ordinary living with an extraordinary God."

— **Kav Rees**, BestReads-kav.blogspot.com

*Where the Heart Is Series*

## Praise for the Where the Heart Is Series

"*Risking Love* is a touching story of love and loss - and risking your heart! I can't wait to read the next in the series!"

—**Regina Rudd Merrick**, author of *Carolina Dream*

"Brenda does a great job bringing us into the story, capturing our attention and keeping it till the end. I read the first book in this series and look forward to the next. I highly recommend *Capturing Beauty* – it's an inspiring story of second chances and new perspectives!"

—**Angela D. Meyer**, author of *Where Hope Starts*

"*Planting Hope* is a lovely wrap-up to the Where the Heart Is series. The strength, or lack thereof, of a family unit has a profound impact on all of its members. Brenda Anderson expertly illustrates that in this story, and all of her books, as she deals honestly with the idiosyncrasies of families – the good, bad, and ugly. *Planting Hope* is about the hope God plants deep in our hearts, and the lengths we'll go to for those we love."

—Award-winning author, **Stacy Monson**,
author of *Open Circle*

If you enjoyed stories by **Brenda S. Anderson**,
you may also enjoy books by **Stacy Monson**

*and the*

Chain of Lakes Series

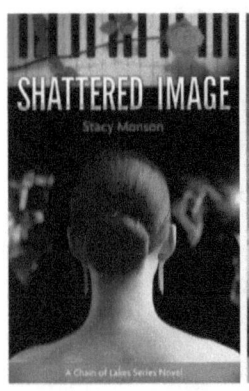

**Brenda S. Anderson** writes gritty and authentic, life-affirming fiction. She is a member of the American Christian Fiction Writers, and is Past-President of the ACFW Minnesota chapter, MN-NICE, the 2016 ACFW Chapter of the Year. When not reading or writing, she enjoys music, theater, roller coasters, and baseball (Go Twins!), and she loves watching movies with her family. She resides in the Minneapolis, Minnesota area with her husband of 31 years, their three children, and one sassy cat.

## Connect with Brenda

**Email**: Brenda@BrendaAndersonBooks.com

**Website**: www.BrendaAndersonBooks.com

**Newsletter**: http://brendaandersonbooks.com/subscribe/

**Facebook**: facebook.com/BrendaSAndersonAuthor/

**Twitter**: twitter.com/BrendaSAnders_n

**Pinterest**: pinterest.com/brendabanderson/

**Goodreads**: goodreads.com/BrendaSAnderson

**BookBub**: bookbub.com/authors/brenda-s-anderson

www.ingramcontent.com/pod-product-compliance
Lightning Source LLC
Chambersburg PA
CBHW030647110726
47901CB00002B/610